Desire Rising

by

Elizabeth Shore

Desire Rising

Contact Information: info@thewildrosepress.com

Cover Art by Debbie Taylor

The Wild Rose Press, Inc.
PO Box 708
Adams Basin, NY 14410-0708

Visit us at www.thewilderroses.com

Publishing History
First Scarlet Rose Edition, 2016
Print ISBN 978-1-5092-0707-7
Digital ISBN 978-1-5092-0708-4

Published in the United States of America

Shedding tragedy can put a heart at risk, but sometimes from desire rises true love…

A low rumble of thunder echoed in the distance. The wind picked up, swirling around them, blowing stray curls of Catherine's hair about her face. She lifted a hand to move aside the wayward strands, but Miles was quicker, stroking his fingers along her cheek, parting her hair from her face as he did so. His touch was soft, delicate, as though handling rare and exorbitantly expensive silk.

Catherine's voice caught in her throat as tingles of arousal stirred the path his fingers traced. He was presumptuous to put his hands about her this way, so intimately, mere minutes after they met. But his seductive aura nearly disarmed her. It was as unthinkable to restrain him as it would be not to breathe. Shivers of anticipation dappled her skin as she allowed him to continue for a moment, closing her eyes.

He tucked the dark strands of her hair behind her ear, his fingers lingering along the curve at the top before at last, with apparent reluctance, drawing his hand away.

More thunder, this time louder. He darted a quick glance at the sky before returning his gaze to her.

"Let us not go in just yet."

"No," she agreed.

It was as if the exchange of words, though merely an agreement on whether to return to the ball, was in fact mutual acknowledgement both wanted something more to happen between them.

Dedication

For Mom. I sure miss our natters.

Chapter One

Kingsbridge, England, 1776

With a deep sigh of pure bliss, Lucy Underhill snuggled beneath the covers, a steaming cup of tea on the night table beside her. Brimming with anticipation, she opened the book of poetry she'd wanted to read for months and set it on her lap. Such a rarity to have the evening to herself! She was as excited as a child with a bag of sweetmeats.

Outside her window, she heard the faint rustle of wind through the trees and the soft patter of late summer rain. She read the first stanza, drawn in by the lilting, hypnotic rhythm of the words. Then without warning, the hairs on the back of her neck shot straight up. Something was outside; she was sure of it.

Like an animal sensing danger, she lifted her head and cocked an ear toward the door, straining for any indication her heartless swine of a husband had returned home. At first there was nothing, only the hushed quiet of a house settling in for the evening. But she couldn't shake the sense she was no longer alone.

The door to her room slammed open with such force that the iron handle dented the wall. Framed by the doorway, John towered, a deep, angry scowl lining his face. For a moment he simply stood and stared, weaving like a listing boat. Then, as if all at once remembering what he'd come there to do, he kicked the door shut and charged. "Show me yer tits, you filthy tart."

Lucy scooted across the bed. "Keep away from me!"

"Whore!" John swiped at her leg. "You'll spread those thighs for any bastard who asks, but you're cold as a fish to me."

"John, please." She uttered her plea with a forced note of calm in an effort to tame the savage beast who was her husband. She stood on the opposite side of the bed, her bare feet icy cold against the floor. With her arms folded protectively across her chest, she clutched at the sleeves of her nightgown and cast John a dreading eye.

It was impossible to know what had prompted his outrage, but the reason mattered not. He'd think of her whatever he liked. He always had. Her only concern now was how to escape.

"Over here. On your knees." Turning back toward Lucy, he tugged at his breeches, the movement made clumsy by the amount of drink in his veins. "May as well get something out of this accursed night," he muttered, still fumbling with the buttons.

So that was it. He'd lost at cards—again—and was taking his anger out on her. Lucy would have none of it.

"Good night, John." She hoped he wouldn't notice the tremor in her voice as she skirted past him, heading for the doorway.

Like so many times before, she assumed that after grumbling in frustration John would pass out in her bed. She'd then spend the remainder of the evening tucked away in his bedroom several paces down the hall.

Just as she reached the door, John gripped her

upper arm and jerked her back toward him. Lucy spun, arms reeling to catch her balance, but the momentum from his sudden action sent them tumbling into the bed. Air whooshed from her lungs as her overfed husband landed squarely on top of her.

"Get away!" She shoved at his bulk, attempting to free herself.

His massive weight jammed her against the mattress like a boulder atop her chest. Arms flailing, she heaved against him, grunting with effort. She bucked her hips, desperate to free herself from her stinking wretch of a husband, but the efforts failed. Try as she might, she could no more move him than an ant could move a mountain.

Seizing his advantage, John's sour breath drifted across her face as he wheezed, "Come now, my sweet. Open those ripe lips and give me what I want."

His breeches were loose, and while lying atop Lucy, he shook them free so they fell from his legs to a heap upon the floor. No longer restricted, he pinned Lucy's arms onto the bed while inching up her body until he could straddle her face and dangle his limp member before her lips.

"Suck," he commanded, wiggling his buttocks so his sex swung to and fro, as if to entice her.

Lucy clamped her lips shut and shook her head, struggling furiously to get out from beneath him. The noxious odor of his cock and balls sickened her, and bile rose in her throat at the thought of having to pleasure him.

"Do it," he growled, lowering himself so the saggy wrinkled foreskin of his cock brushed Lucy's lips.

She turned her head as far away as she could

manage while still thrashing about, trying to rid herself of the oaf. Her refusal would enrage him, but she would not succumb to his demands. Not again.

He roared with anger and slapped her hard, striking the side of her cheek against her teeth and breaking the skin inside her mouth. A trickle of blood oozed between her lips.

Paying no heed to her injury, John pressed his advantage, using his knees to pin down her arms. With both of his palms splayed on either side of her face, he steadied her head to position it just beneath his dangling cock. He pressed his thumbs against her lips, attempting to pry them open.

Blind fury pumped through Lucy's veins. She would not have this horrid, sweaty, disgusting pile of offal force her into doing one more thing against her will. It mattered not that he was her husband; after two long years of this behavior, she'd had enough.

With every ounce of strength she possessed, Lucy brought her head forward like a medieval battering ram and slammed it into John's balls.

"Son of a whore!" he screamed, clutching his groin and rolling to his side.

In a split second, Lucy scampered off the bed. The door was straight ahead, her escape hatch from hell. Her feet touched the floor and she took a single step, fleeing toward sanctuary.

The vise-like grip of John's hand in her hair stopped her cold.

"No!" Her cries filled the room as he reeled her back toward him, hapless as a fish on a line. She jerked violently against his hold, ignoring the searing pain as strands of her hair ripped from her scalp. No amount of struggling would get her free, and she stumbled backward as John pulled her to where he sat on the side of the bed. She fell into his lap and he wrapped his arms around her waist. She writhed against his grip, shrieking in frustration.

"Oh, so you like it rough, do you, Lucy?" he growled in her ear, smothering her in a toxic cloud of hot, fetid breath.

"Let go of me!" She turned toward him and swung out, aiming anywhere on his body to hurt him.

Her fingers curled in a fist as her arm whipped around like a weighted pendulum and suddenly connected with the side of his bloated face. A brittle crack rent the air as bone connected with bone, Lucy's fist on her husband's jaw. A bolt of pain roared through her hand. She cried out, shaking her throbbing fingers.

"Damnation, you bloody bitch!"

His eyes had narrowed to slits but flashed with stark raving fury. Terror clenched her heart like a fist from hell. Jerking hard against him, she at last broke free and flew across the room. John bellowed like an enraged bull. Lucy twisted the handle, swung the door open, and chanced a look back to see how closely he followed.

John shoved himself up and away from the bed. He took a step, attempting to give chase, when his feet became tangled in the discarded heap of his trousers still lying on the floor.

"Ah!" His cry echoed in the room as he lost balance while struggling to free himself.

He fell forward, toward the fireplace, arms uselessly pinwheeling as his temple caught the edge of the marble mantel. Breath whooshed from his lungs.

His knees buckled and he sank, striking his head sharply against the unforgiving stone hearth. The crack of his skull was like the brittle snap of breaking winter ice. He lay where he'd fallen, immobile, his eyes wide open in an unseeing stare, his lips parted but silent.

Shivers of horror froze the blood in Lucy's veins. Gripping fistfuls of her nightgown with shaking fingers, she stood rooted in place as if trapped in an inconceivable tableau vivant, doomed to be forever linked to this terrifying moment. Time ceased movement. The spell finally broke when a crimson pool of blood began seeping out from beneath John's head, and she could at last tear away her gaze.

She let out a long breath and steeled herself, knowing what she had to do. With grim determination, she walked back to the bed and pulled off the linens. Her hands were curiously steady as she wrapped her now deceased husband's bleeding head in a well-spun white cotton sheet. It had been a wedding gift, she remembered. Now it was John's burial shroud.

The click of a heel made her start. Lucy turned, knowing before seeing her that it would be the housekeeper, Mrs. Tuckett. The wise, older woman assessed the situation with a single swift look.

"We'll need to get him in the ground quick, before anyone else sees," she said, her sharp blue eyes gazing intently at Lucy. A strand of powder white hair free of its daytime bun peeked out from beneath her nightcap and fell softly against her aging cheek. Absently she tucked it back behind her ear as she stepped into the room and closed the door behind her.

"It was an accident, Mrs. Tuckett. I didn't—"

"'Course it was an accident. You're not that kind

of woman, my lady." The housekeeper crouched down to the pile of bed linens on the floor and picked up a blanket to wrap it around John, her expression stern. "Not that I'd blame you if you were."

Lucy lifted her gaze in stunned surprise at the soft-spoken housekeeper's cold, acerbic tone. Mrs. Tuckett pressed her lips tight as set about her task. Her movements were quick and efficient, making no effort to be gentle. In silent understanding, the women worked as one to wrap the body.

When they finished, Mrs. Tuckett straightened and cast her gaze toward the door.

"I don't hear anything out there, my lady. But let me go make certain no one's up and about. I'll only be a moment."

The night was still pitch dark with dawn yet hours away. More importantly, despite Lucy's screams of protest during their struggle, the servants had not stirred to help. John ruled his household by fear and intimidation, and his staff knew any attempt to interfere would result in nothing less than their immediate dismissal.

Seconds later, the housekeeper returned. "All is quiet, my lady," she said. "Let's bring the body outside."

"You needn't get involved," Lucy replied. "I can handle this on my own."

"Begging no disrespect, my lady, but you can no more handle it on your own than you could take wing and fly to the sun. Lord Underhill must weigh a good seventeen, maybe eighteen stone. You ain't getting him outta here by yourself." She leaned down to grasp the end of the sheet at John's head. "If you take hold o' that end, we can drag him across the floor and—"

The slam of fists on the front door downstairs stopped her cold.

"You cock-sucking mongrel, John, where'd you run off to? You promised me a good fuck with that whore wife of yours, so let me in!" The doorknob rattled with violent force as the outsider attempted to enter. "By the balls, *now*! Damnation, open the door!"

Mrs. Tuckett turned eyes as wide as dish plates toward Lucy. "Sweet heaven, it's Mr. Underhill."

As horribly as John had treated her, he was nearly kind compared to his black-hearted, violent brother, Simon. The younger sibling had always despised Lucy, viewing her as nothing more than a calculating opportunist who'd tricked his brother into marriage for his money and title. Nothing could be further from the truth, but Simon refused to see it any other way.

"He'll have you hanged if he sees his brother dead," Mrs. Tuckett whispered as Simon's pounding grew louder. "Quick. Hide the body."

"Where?" Lucy pleaded, her voice choked with fear. "Simon will see him."

"Not if I still draw breath he won't." The housekeeper's jaw was set, her face a mask of resolve. "Shove him under the bed."

"It's the first place he'll look."

Mrs. Tuckett flipped aside a lock of hair that had pried itself loose from her nightcap. "Then we'll have to make sure that doesn't happen." A faint tremble crept into the housekeeper's voice, and she swallowed hard, as if devouring her fear.

Her sharp gaze scanned the room before returning to Lucy. "Besides, there's nowhere else to put him and no time before Simon breaks the door down. Now be quick, mistress. Grab hold of that end and *pull*."

Though John's bulk was massive, the blanket wrappings made it possible for the women to slide his body across the wooden floor and squeeze it beneath the bed frame. Once finished, they raced around the bed, arranging the quilt so it acted as a curtain, hiding the space beneath the frame.

"Damn your prick to hell!" Simon bellowed from below. "Let me in!"

Lucy swiped away the sweat trickling down her temples and nodded at Mrs. Tuckett.

"You'd best answer the door," she said above the thunderous slamming of her heartbeat. "I shall be in bed, just as I was minutes ago. Tell Simon that John never arrived home. We've not seen nor heard from him since he left earlier this eve."

Simon's commotion had at last caused the other servants to stir. Their confused mutterings echoed outside the hallway.

"Attend to the others." Lucy squeezed the housekeeper's hand as Mrs. Tuckett prepared to exit. "And thank you."

"You're the only good thing that's ever happened in this household," Mrs. Tuckett replied, her eyes meeting Lucy's in an unflinching gaze. "That heartless cur got what he deserved." Then she spun on her heel and left the bedroom, closing the door behind her.

Lucy dove into bed. If John hadn't returned home she surely would have been sleeping by this time, so that's what she pretended to do. She snuffed out the candle, settling beneath the covers as darkness filtered in.

Directly below her lay the corpse of her dead husband. She shuddered as icy tingles of fear crawled down her back. Despite ordering herself not to think of it, her mind disobeyed, like an errant child refusing to listen.

Images of John's wide, startled eyes followed by the crack of his skull on the floor repeated over and over in a never-ending nightmare of horror. Lucy squeezed her eyes shut, trying to block the memories and instead focus on the conversation below.

"You can't go up there!" The heavy thud of boot steps on the stairs followed Mrs. Tuckett's angry voice.

"Out of my way, woman," Simon roared. "I'll do as I please."

Like a repeat of earlier in the evening, seconds later the door flew open. Lucy didn't have to pretend when her heart lurched in her throat, and she let out a startled scream. She snatched at the bedcovers and pushed herself up to a half sitting position.

"What are you doing here?" she gasped as Simon stalked toward the bed.

"Where's my brother, you conniving bitch?" He raised a lantern to light the room and cast his gaze about.

He was a large man, well over six foot two, his chest like a barrel and his huge beefy hands capable of choking her life out in seconds if he so desired. Lucy swallowed, trying to quell her trembling.

"I— I don't know what you mean. I've been asleep. Perhaps he's—"

"Don't lie to me. He said he was going home."

"You'll be treating my lady with respect," Mrs. Tuckett demanded from where she stood in the doorway. "We haven't seen Lord Underhill since he left earlier this eve. He ain't been home, and that's the truth of it."

"The truth of it, eh?" Paying no mind to the lateness of the hour he stomped about the room, peering behind large items of furniture and opening then slamming closed the armoire doors.

"John," he bellowed. "Where the devil are you?"

He stood, rooted in place, head cocked to the side as if listening for his brother. His massive frame filled the room and sucked the air out of it.

Lucy felt as if she were being suffocated. Her shaking, clammy fingers clutched the bed sheet to her chin as her heartbeat thundered like cannon shots. All at once Simon turned, facing Lucy directly, his shiny lips upturned in a sly grin.

"I just realized where he's hiding." He chuckled, mock-slapping his forehead as if chastising his own stupidity. "Of course. He's under the bed."

Icy terror knifed Lucy's heart. Helpless as a prisoner, she watched Simon crouch down and cup his hands in a ring around his mouth. "Come out from under there, you son of a whore," he called, his booming voice echoing about the room.

He listened for a moment before taking steps forward, edging ever closer to the bed.

"You got no business in here," Mrs. Tuckett insisted, her voice rising. "If you want to see for yourself, sir, why don't you have a look around the stable? Your brother's mount will be there if he's home."

The housekeeper's suggestion seemed to strike the younger brother as amusing. An oily smile turned the corners of his lips.

"Well now," he said, his attention riveted to Lucy. "A 'mount' is just what I'm aiming for. John made a bet and lost it. A fuck from his wife is my prize. I came to collect."

The shock from his vulgar statement was shadowed only by Lucy's icy fear that he'd catch sight of John's body. A boulder of panic lodged deep in her throat. Her limbs felt heavy as trees, pinning her to the bed.

The dark secret in that room was seconds away from discovery, and she'd be seconds away from being hanged for murder if she didn't stop Simon from finding his dead brother beneath the bed. With Herculean effort, she dredged up her last remaining shred of courage and flung off the bed sheet.

Her movement stopped Simon's advance and, with a gleam in his eyes, he watched as she slid from the bed and took a step toward him.

"We told you, sir, that my lord husband hasn't yet returned home," she said softly, fluttering her eyelashes. "But that doesn't mean you can't collect what's owed to you, does it?"

"Well," Simon growled, his groping fingers reaching out to trace a path along Lucy's bare arm. "That's more like it."

She fought back a shudder of revulsion and forced herself to smile up at him.

"Mrs. Tuckett," she said, keeping her gaze locked to Simon's. "My lord's brother has had a hard ride here and needs refreshment. Bring us wine, if you please."

The housekeeper's faint voice was stained with disbelief. "Wine, my lady?"

"Yes. Right away." For a brief moment, Lucy

glanced straight at Mrs. Tuckett. "Bring that vintage we reserve for special occasions. The one I sometimes give my lord husband."

The corners of Mrs. Tuckett's mouth lifted in a shadow of a smile before she pressed her lips together and turned away. It was enough for Lucy to catch a glimmer of hope. The housekeeper knew what she wanted.

When the door clicked closed she returned her attention to Simon. Ignoring the sudden heave of her stomach, she ran her fingertips along his arm. "How warm you must be, sir, from that fierce ride," she cooed. "Let's get you out of this coat."

"Ah, but you're a wanton little whore." Simon shrugged off the garment and tossed it on a nearby chair. "Just as John said you'd be." His movements now less restricted, he swatted Lucy's buttocks to direct her toward the bed.

Fire-hot rage burned through her veins, and it was all she could do not to crack her palm hard across Simon's smug face. A sudden rap on the door helped her fight back the urge.

"Yes?"

"It's Mrs. Tuckett, my lady," the housekeeper said behind the door. "I've come with the wine."

"You may enter."

The door swung open, and Mrs. Tuckett stepped inside, her arms laden with a silver tray holding two goblets of red wine and a platter of fruit. She set the tray atop the nightstand.

"It's just the one you requested, my lady," she said. "The special vintage."

Lucy walked over to where the housekeeper stood,

purposely inserting herself between the bed and Mrs. Tuckett to block Simon's view of the tray. Mrs. Tuckett lifted one of the wine goblets and placed it in Lucy's hand, lightly tapping her index finger against the glass. Lucy knew what the signal meant. That was the goblet for Simon.

She gave the housekeeper a subtle nod and then turned away, wine glasses in her hand.

"That will be all, Mrs. Tuckett. Thank you."

"As you please, my lady." The housekeeper's soft steps carried her out of the room and she shut the door behind her. Lucy plastered a giant smile across her face and beamed at Simon, hoping he wouldn't notice how her hands shook.

"Here you are, sir," she said, giving him a glass. "'Tis our finest vintage. Your brother only lets me serve it to our most important guests."

"Does he, now?" Simon chuckled as he took a sip. For a moment he grimaced and Lucy's heart stopped. If Simon noticed something amiss with the wine, her plan would be ruined.

She took a sip from her own glass. "Truthfully, I did not care for it at first," she lied. "It tasted queer. But John had scolded me for my coarseness and had told me he expected a silly goose like me not to understand fine wine." She giggled at her supposed foolishness and took another sip. "But I'm certain a cultured man such as yourself would appreciate it."

Puffed up with self-importance, Simon nodded and emptied his glass in a single swallow. "Of course I do. But enough with the drinking." Placing his goblet on the nightstand, he turned toward Lucy with a lecherous grin curling his lips. "On to the fucking!"

He sat down on the bed and pulled her along with him. As he held her atop his body, his splayed palm cupped the back of Lucy's head, and he brought her face toward his. For one vile moment she smelled the rancid odor of his breath—a potent combination of garlic sausage and beer—before his greasy lips fused themselves to hers, smothering her with the foul taste of his tongue jammed in her mouth.

Her stomach heaved and she fought down the gag. Her chance of escape would die if she pretended anything less than complete rapture.

"Sir Simon," she breathed, at last able to break away from his mouth. "You're ablaze!"

"Sure I am, for a horny wench like you," he mumbled, sucking on her neck.

Lucy noticed his movements were slowing. His arms slid from her body. She held her breath, scarcely daring to hope. Simon's lips were no longer against her throat and his head had dropped back on the pillow. She glanced over and saw his eyes were closed. At last, the drugged wine was working.

Still lying atop him, she remained immobile, her body like stone. A minute passed, then another. Simon's breathing deepened, becoming slow and even. And then Lucy heard a sound more glorious than a choir of heavenly angels—the deep rumbling of Simon's snores. She eased herself into a sitting position and slid from the bed.

Her bare feet were whisper silent as she raced over to the door and flung it open.

In seconds, Mrs. Tuckett appeared. "He's out?"

Lucy nodded.

"It'll be hours, then," the housekeeper affirmed,

glancing over at the snoring Simon. "I gave him enough laudanum to sink a horse."

The relief surging through Lucy transformed to cold fear. There was still so much to do.

"We must bury the body," she stated, panic rising. "Quickly, while Simon sleeps."

She rushed to the bed, flipped aside the quilt, and reached underneath to grasp hold of the blanket covering John. But before she could even begin to pull, Mrs. Tuckett stopped her with a firm hand atop her shoulder.

"My lady, listen to me. 'Tis foolishness, it is, to be wasting precious time. I'll take care of Lord John, don't you worry yourself about it. Right now, you need to prepare."

Lucy halted her progress, frowning. "Prepare? What do you mean?"

Mrs. Tuckett said quietly, "You know what I mean."

Unexpected tears burned Lucy's eyes. She did know what the housekeeper meant and what had to be done. Shoving aside her fear, she nodded. "I cannot stay."

"Of course not. You'll never be safe from Simon. Once he discovers his brother is dead, you'll be blamed for murder. And what chance have you to fight it?"

What chance indeed. Lucy's poor, untitled family was powerless against the Underhill's wealthy nobility. Simon would have revenge for his brother's death, and Lucy would be hanged. How ironic that the arranged marriage when she was just sixteen, meant to give her advantages she'd otherwise never have, had turned into the nightmare of her life. She had to get away.

"Do you have somewhere you could go, my lady? Someone who would keep you safe?"

Did she? Until mere minutes ago, her world had revolved around John's. His friends, his family, his life. What had she of her own? Who could she trust with her dangerous secret? Lucy's mind spun. Then, suddenly, she had her answer.

Lightning quick, Lucy entered John's private study and helped herself to the entire contents of his personal storage chest—jewelry, coins, important papers, everything. She'd sort through it later and discard what she didn't need. But now, with time ticking, she merely dumped it all in a leather travel pack to carry away.

Returning to her bedchamber, she ignored Simon's rumbling snores—and the body of her dead husband tucked beneath the bed—and changed from her sleeping gown into a travel dress and a stout pair of shoes.

Before leaving, she took one last look around. Aside from John's physical and emotional abuse, she had nothing to show from her two years of marriage. Misery was the only thing she'd be leaving behind. Determination stiffened her spine. Time to go.

Mrs. Tuckett awaited her by the back door. The two women locked gazes, and the housekeeper nodded her approval. Then she pressed a small package into her hands, and the comforting aroma of bread and cheese filled the air. Tears shimmered in her eyes.

"Godspeed, my lady," she whispered.

Lucy's throat was so tight she couldn't speak. She squeezed Mrs. Tuckett's aging yet strong hand, signaling a final farewell, and turned away. She quickly and quietly entered the stables and saddled John's finest stallion herself, sending up a grateful prayer that Simon had never come looking for it.

She made so little noise even the stable boy failed to wake. Once outdoors, she swung herself up and into the saddle and then raced into the darkness and away from the madness.

She gripped the reins of the charging stallion, grateful for moonlight that helped guide her way. Chilly evening air nipped at her face and pierced through to her clothing, making her shiver. Her hand still ached. But none of that mattered, because now she was free.

All at once, bubbles of laughter danced through her body, and she laughed out loud as the fresh air cleansed her, blowing away the past. Letting out a whoop of victory, she urged her muscled steed faster as they raced through the night.

Hours later, Lucy looked toward the east and the faintest tinge of pink brushed the horizon. It would be light soon, but Simon would never find her. She'd come up with a plan that just might work to keep herself away from him forever. As the sun's rays peeked out and shone upon another day, they lit a path toward her ultimate destination—Audrey's home—the one place in all the world where she hoped she would be safe.

Chapter Two

London, England, 1780

Tortured groans filled the stately bedchamber as the Earl of Clifton begged for his lover.

"Now," he demanded, his brow beaded with sweat. "I must have you now."

Catherine Sheffield purred with anticipation. "I should hope so, my lord."

He grasped hold of her ankles and wrapped her legs about his waist. As he did so, Catherine reached forward to close her fingers around his cock. She swirled the head around the entrance to her sex, moistening him with her juices. Clifton groaned in ecstasy and drove into her.

The pace of his coupling quickly grew frenzied, desperate for the release so long denied. He leaned forward, kissing Catherine's lips, her cheeks, her forehead, then farther down, along the slender column of her throat, until finally he sucked her nipples. She arched against him, her hips raised to meet each one of his ardent thrusts. At last, Clifton could hold off no longer and, with a delirious roar, spilled his seed.

For several long moments they lay collapsed upon the bed, able to do nothing more than get their breathing under control.

"Ye Gods, you'll be the death of me," Clifton groaned, extricating himself from tangled limbs to begin assembling his clothing.

It was his most ardent expression of praise, and Catherine smiled.

"If that's the case, you had best spend the afternoon at rest."

"In preparation for this eve, you mean?"

She nodded. "I trust you plan on attending the Kenworth ball?"

"Indeed," Clifton affirmed, tugging on a stocking. "As long as you are there, that is."

Still lying in bed, Catherine propped herself up against the numerous plush pillows thrown about the mattress. She enjoyed Clifton's bedchamber. Perhaps some found its ostentatious décor overbearing, but she appreciated the luxurious fabrics and bold colors.

She stretched like a cat upon the dark green bedcover, not in the least intimidated by the fact that Clifton was fully dressed while she wore nothing at all. Still, she couldn't hold off a faint frown. Clifton was becoming possessive, a sure sign it was time for their relationship to end.

"George."

The Earl turned to look at her, and she heard his breath hitch in his throat.

"As many times as we have been together, I am still startled by your beauty."

"As I am appreciative of your kind words," she replied, touched by his compliment. "Yet..."

"What is it?"

"I'm certain you won't take offense when I tell you we shall both enjoy ourselves more this evening knowing neither of us is attached to the other."

"Not attached? But I thought—"

"You are more than kind for offering to escort me. But 'tis not necessary."

Clifton stayed silent a moment, likely digesting her words, and Catherine granted him time. She was, after all, concluding their relationship. A pity but most definitely required.

Clifton cleared his throat and gave Catherine a short nod. "I have enjoyed your company," he said, "and it is with reluctance we are now to part."

"I would never presume to occupy too much time with such an esteemed gentleman as yourself, my lord. Not with so many other ladies vying for a chance at a proposal of marriage."

"But you—"

"Are not one of those ladies."

She could not have been more clear had she hung a sign 'round her neck, but it was a matter of pride for her to end relationships with style and grace. It allowed her and her lover to part as friends.

"Very well, then." He peered in the looking glass and gave his cravat a final straightening tug. "In that case perhaps I shall go for a smoke at Tom's. You are welcome to stay here for as long as you wish. I shall have my driver take you home."

"Thank you, but 'tis unnecessary. My own driver awaits me just around the corner."

"Ah. Of course. I don't know why my memory slipped." He gave her a wry grin. "Catherine Sheffield is obliged to no one."

"I prefer to say no one is under obligation to me."

"Whether we wish it or not."

Clifton tipped his hat to her and with a short bow left the room. When she could no longer hear his footsteps echoing down the hall, Catherine released a contented sigh. Clifton was certainly a charming man, but it was time for him to go. She knew what it was like when a man became too attached to her, too possessive. And she'd vowed long ago it would never happen again.

****

The lilting strains of an English country dance floated about the room, permeating the air in a faint yet noticeable way. The participants gathered in the center of the ballroom floor grasped hands to step together, then draw apart, twirling about each other like flowers caught in the eddy of a stream. Expensive pipe smoke and even more expensive perfume lingered in the air, their cloying essence hovering about the guests like an overly attentive butler.

Miles Hawkins stood in the far corner of the room and clenched his jaw, stifling a bored yawn. His eyelids were heavy as shutters, longing to be drawn closed for the night. He'd bet ten quid that James Norris, standing beside him, felt exactly the same. Finishing his third whisky of the evening with an impatient toss down his throat, his friend snapped his fingers signaling for more.

"'Tis the only way to endure these," he advised as a stoic waiter exchanged his empty glass for a full one. "Believe me, Hawkins, you'll remember again soon enough."

Miles raised his eyebrow but remained silent. He'd never been prone to idle chatter, and since the trauma in his life some two years past, he had become a man of even fewer words. He took comfort that Norris knew him well and would not demand an evening of lively banter. Miles had only recently begun to venture back into society, and his friend proved himself invaluable in reacquainting Miles with those of rank and stature.

They glanced around the room, nodding to friends and engaging in polite conversation with those who stopped to chat. While Miles half-listened to an extremely droll Henry Perdsworth ramble on about his latest battle with gout, his attention became riveted to the elegant, raven-hair woman passing through the doorway. Even from his vantage point several feet away, her slightly slanted cat eyes and flawless pale skin mesmerized him.

"Who is she?" he demanded in a quiet voice to Norris.

His friend looked up. "Her name is Catherine Sheffield." He and Miles excused themselves and stepped away from the group with whom they'd been speaking in order to gain a moment of privacy.

"She's the niece and sole heir of Lady Audrey Sheffield," Norris continued. "I know naught of her parents, though it is said they've passed, and Miss Sheffield uses no title. There's not much more about her known beyond that."

Miles could not take his eyes off of her. "Introduce me."

Norris nodded agreement but made no comment. If he was surprised by the degree of Miles' interest, he kept the thought to himself.

They wove their way toward the front of the room, carefully avoiding the clusters of ladies gathered next to one another as if conspiring against the woman who stood out among the rest. Catherine seemed indifferent by the subtle evasion of those few, her focus instead on the Duke and Duchess of Kenworth, hosts of the party.

As he and Norris approached, he caught part of the conversation.

"The room sparkles as always under your elegant touch, Your Grace," Catherine complimented the duchess. "The orchids you grow are particularly beautiful."

The duchess nodded, her diamond headband catching the light and glittering like snowflakes in her graying hair. "And you, Catherine, appear to be the only one who has noticed."

"Perhaps it is simply that the others are too overwhelmed to comment."

"Too lazy, more likely."

Miles grinned. The duchess had a reputation for speaking her mind.

"But I care naught," the duchess continued. "The orchids please me, and so I am content. You go on now and enjoy yourself. 'Twould appear you have admirers already."

At the duchess' comment, Catherine turned to where Norris and Miles stood only a few feet away. Miles nodded politely and saw out of the corner of his eye his friend doing the same.

Catherine turned away from the duchess to descend the few stairs leading from the entryway to the ballroom below, her fitted silk gown following the elegant contour of her slim silhouette.

As she approached them, Norris captured her hand and swept a kiss across her knuckles. For a few seconds he said nothing, appearing content to simply admire her. Then a rakish grin crinkled his features. "As always, I am stunned into silence by your beauty."

Catherine laughed, her eyes sparkling with humor.

"Do you never run out of ways to amuse me?"

"I sincerely hope not, though I was serious just now. You are lovely this evening, Catherine."

"And you, Sir James, are more than kind."

Norris turned and nodded to acknowledge his friend. "Let me introduce you to Lord Miles Hawkins. Miles, may I present Miss Catherine Sheffield."

Miles stepped forward and clasped her hand in his, wrapping her soft, cool fingers in the heat of his palm. For a brief moment, he dropped gentlemanly reserves and pierced her with his stare, drinking her in. She was even more lovely up close, where flecks of gold danced amid the ivy green of her eyes. Her scent drifted toward him, something subtle and refined, lavender perhaps. He breathed in as if to bottle the fragrance in his memory.

A single strand of dark glossy hair brushed her cheek and an urge to step closer, to draw her toward him and bury his face in that thick mane seized him. His blood spiked and raced straight to his groin. He clenched his jaw, suppressing a groan.

He lowered his head and brushed a kiss across her hand. "Miss Sheffield," he murmured. "'Tis a pleasure."

A playful smile danced about her lips. "Likewise, I am certain."

Miles released her hand with reluctance, although noted her initial cool touch had grown warm. And when she'd spoken just now, he was certain he'd heard a soft hitch in her breath. Was she as similarly affected by their contact? The thought oddly pleased him, and he stepped back to resume his place beside Norris.

A waiter approached, bearing glasses of

Champagne upon a silver tray. They each accepted one and then distanced themselves from the entrance so as not to impede the arriving guests.

Catherine turned to Norris. "Tell me, James. Why is it Lord Miles and I have never before met? I thought I knew all your friends by now."

"You very nearly do," Norris agreed. "But Miles has been...away and is just now returning to the social scene."

"Then I shall wish you a warm welcome back," Catherine replied, not pressing.

"Clearly there is much I have missed," he stated, once more capturing her in his gaze. To his surprise—and fascination—a hint of pink stained her cheeks.

The ballroom filled with a heavy influx of guests, causing the temperature to soar. Catherine reached into the small satin bag tied about her waist, extracted her fan, and shook it open, sweeping silk folds through the heated air. She released a contented sigh as the cool, gentle currents blew tendrils of hair from her face.

"The Kenworth ball never fails to draw the season's largest crowd," Norris observed, glancing around.

As Catherine turned toward him to comment, Miles embraced the opportunity to study her.

Her irrefutable beauty captivated him. Taller than most women, her extraordinary appearance burned a lasting image in his mind, like seeing a rare or exotic orchid for the very first time.

But beyond mere looks her elegant confidence and unshakeable sense of self were what Miles found indisputably erotic. The graceful way in which she'd turned a potentially awkward moment—Norris' vague explanation of Miles being "away"—into an opportunity to welcome him was unexpected and wildly intriguing and so unlike the behavior of most women he'd met. No persistent questions or sly manipulations to get him to reveal details about himself he'd rather keep hidden. Beautiful, self-assured. His imagination took flight as he pictured her in bed, and a surge of arousal shot straight to his groin.

"Why, Sir James, is that you?" A squeaky female voice pierced the air, and they turned to greet the petite blonde who approached.

"The Honorable Elaine Palmer," Norris announced, the forced enthusiasm in his voice causing a corner of Miles' lips to lift in a faint grin. He knew his friend struggled not to roll his eyes at the girl's arrival, the eldest daughter of a local baron who had tried unsuccessfully for years to get herself betrothed to him. And if Norris had anything to say about it, Miss Palmer's pursuits would forever end in disappointment.

Norris greeted her with a chaste kiss on her hand and introduced his friends. Elaine gave only the barest of nods to Catherine, but she smiled coyly when introduced to Miles.

"How dreadful we've not had the pleasure of meeting before now, Lord Miles." She pouted prettily, fluttering her lashes. "I insist you join me for glass of Champagne."

"Alas, but I must decline your invitation," Miles replied, suddenly realizing he'd been handed a most pleasurable opportunity. "I was just escorting Miss Sheffield outside for air. Please excuse us."

Without awaiting Miss Palmer's reply, Miles placed a light hand on Catherine's elbow and steered her through the welter of guests.

****

The combination of Miles' height and good looks cleared a path before them, and in no time, Catherine found herself led out on to the balcony to enjoy the breezy, evening air. Heat from Miles' hand burned an arousing path along her arm. Her skin prickled with awareness of his presence, noting the alluring way his muscles flexed as he guided her beside him, evident even beneath the sleeve of his coat.

He'd captured her interest from the moment they'd met, drawing her in with his unapologetic gaze, so intently focused on no one but her. He'd captivated her with surprising ease and she willingly followed where he led, eager to spend time with this arousing, seductive man.

Miles closed the doors behind him, muffling the ballroom din to distant strains of music accompanying the soft rustle of wind in the trees. Other couples were kept at bay by the approaching dinner hour, allowing Miles and her to stroll alone. Candles in large glass containers to shield their flames from the wind were placed intermittently along the balcony floor, lighting a path in the warm, dark night.

As silence descended comfortably between them, Catherine's mind flashed back to the incident prompting their outdoor escape. Seconds later, she struggled not to smile, but she knew the effort failed when Miles spoke up.

"Tell me, Miss Sheffield. What has you so amused?"

She chuckled softly. "It is not my usual style to take pleasure at another's expense, yet I cannot help it. I do not believe I have ever before seen such a look of outrage on anyone's face."

"You refer to Miss Palmer?"

"Indeed. You slighted her quite dreadfully."

"I did, yes."

His swift acknowledgement surprised her. "Do you not think it was perhaps a bit harsh?"

They had reached the far end of the balcony, but rather than round the corner to continue walking, Miles stopped and rested against the stone wall. He released Catherine's arm and turned her to face him.

"'Tis no less than what she did to you." His quiet voice held an undercurrent of steel.

She regarded him calmly, although her tranquil exterior masked the curious racing of her heart. *Heaven above, the man is attractive*. Over the years she'd known her share of eye-catching men, but Miles Hawkins exceeded the most exquisite by far.

With a subtle glance beneath hooded lashes, she took him in. His long, lean frame resembled that of a panther's, with dangerous looks to match. His face was chiseled, his features seemingly etched from stone. He wore no wig and rich, sable hair brushed atop his shoulders. His brown, fathomless eyes surveyed his surroundings with an air of slight detachment, but it served to heighten the enigmatic mystery about him. Why on Earth was the man unwed? Or was he?

She suddenly realized she'd not been informed of his marital status. An oversight, perhaps, or another detail he chose not to reveal? With each passing minute, her fascination grew. Even his gallantry intrigued her. There'd been no need for him to take action against young Elaine Palmer's silly rebuff, yet Catherine found herself oddly pleased he'd done so nonetheless.

"I am not put out by foolish young girls," she at last responded.

"Nor would it occur to me that you are. But I abhor the assumption that those of rank are entitled to poor behavior."

She nodded agreement. "We share the same abhorrence."

For a moment conversation stilled, and she and Miles basked in shared silence. Catherine felt no compulsion to make idle chatter merely to fill the void. Nor apparently did he. Although she'd only just met Miles, they shared a surprising ease.

A low rumble of thunder echoed in the distance. The wind picked up, swirling around them, blowing stray curls of Catherine's hair about her face. She lifted a hand to move aside the wayward strands, but Miles was quicker, stroking his fingers along her cheek, parting her hair from her face as he did so. His touch was soft, delicate, as though handling rare and exorbitantly expensive silk.

Catherine's voice caught in her throat as tingles of arousal stirred the path his fingers traced. He was presumptuous to put his hands about her this way, so intimately, mere minutes after they met. But his seductive aura nearly disarmed her. It was as unthinkable to restrain him as it would be not to breathe. Shivers of anticipation dappled her skin as she allowed him to continue for a moment, closing her eyes.

He tucked the dark strands of her hair behind her ear, his fingers lingering along the curve at the top before at last, with apparent reluctance, drawing his hand away.

More thunder, this time louder. He darted a quick glance at the sky before returning his gaze to her.

"Let us not go in just yet."

"No," she agreed.

It was as if the exchange of words, though merely an agreement on whether to return to the ball, was in fact mutual acknowledgement both wanted something more to happen between them.

Miles' hand, the same one that seconds ago had touched Catherine's face, slipped down to curve around her waist and press lightly against her back. He brought her closer to him, their bodies separated by a smattering of inches. He looked down at her, his considerable height making Catherine feel small and feminine and wildly desired. The warm caress of his breath drifted across her face, the short, ragged exhalations an unspoken indication of his arousal.

It was not quite sane for them to desire one another so strongly and so suddenly, as though cast under a spell. She was also aware of how little she cared. She lived her life to enjoy the rare and spontaneous moments, however inexplicable they may be.

Miles bent down, bringing his face still closer, and in the seconds before his lips captured hers, the depth and haunting beauty of his eyes reflected back at her. Then his mouth was upon hers, stealing her very breath, and she was awash in such blissful sensation that coherent thought became as impossible as taking flight.

He drew back to nibble on her top lip, then her bottom one, his pace agonizingly slow as he teased. Catherine's desire spiked, blood burning through her veins as her pulse raced. She wanted more, but Miles refused to concede, holding off as though he'd ordered himself not to rush. His mouth lingered on hers before he swept the tip of his tongue along her lips, forcing them to part beneath his.

He explored the moist depths as if sampling fine wine. His lips were hot, demanding, and Catherine's passion hovered beyond the boundaries of control. A low groan escaped her lips as her head swam. Miles kissed her mouth, her cheek, along her jaw line, and then he descended, kissing the length of her throat.

She allowed her head to fall back, laying bare her neck, weaving her fingers through Miles' hair as he continued his journey. He trailed his tongue down her throat, dipping into the small hollow at the base, swirling the tip there and then pressing his lips against the tender flesh.

His mouth was so soft, yet so hot, she feared she might melt beneath the sear of his kiss. Her heartbeat was wildly erratic, excited pulses fluttering like the wings of a bird. Miles' hand made a slow, excruciating descent along the length of her spine, his strong fingers caressing every inch of her back as he eased lower and lower still.

When he returned his kisses to her lips, swollen from the ardor of his earlier embrace, Catherine led the kiss. She parted his lips with her tongue, tasting as she pleased like a brazen explorer. Miles groaned into her mouth and pressed his pelvis against hers, the hard bulge of his erection causing a surge of arousal to shoot straight to the sizzling pulses in her core.

She sucked in a breath as he slid his hand down from where it rested atop her shoulder to capture the swell of her breast. Through the silk fabric of her dress he teased, tracing whisper soft swirls along the sides of her breast and around her puckered nipple.

Catherine sank even farther into Miles' embrace, drowning amid the onslaught of sensation like a fishing boat caught in an ocean storm. But then slowly, bit by bit, she eased herself away until at last they parted. She had sampled enough to know what he could give, but here, on the duke and duchess' balcony, was not the place for more.

For an instant lightning lit up the night sky, streaking a flash of color through the air like an artist dashing the first stroke of paint across a canvas. A roar of thunder followed close behind. Rain was at hand.

Catherine took a step back from Miles and, without a shade of embarrassment, calmly smoothed her hair and adjusted her dress. Once she had finished there appeared nothing more to do but join the guests inside for dinner, but Miles seemed reluctant to leave. He stalled by the balcony, and Catherine, sensing there was something he wanted to say, did not press their departure.

For a moment he was quiet, as if testing the words in his mind before he spoke them aloud. Then, in his unreserved manner that was beginning to feel familiar, he said what was on his mind.

"I would see you again."

Catherine had guessed as much. A smile curled her lips. Since parting ways with the Earl of Clifton this afternoon, she was receptive to taking up a new lover. Lord Miles Hawkins, with his exotic, dangerous looks and seductive ways was an obvious choice. Although, as soon as she thought of him as her new lover it felt strangely wrong, as if it diminished what more Miles could be to her.

With hardened resolve, Catherine pushed the thought aside. Years ago, when people knew her as Lucy Underhill, she'd been fooled into believing a man with wealth and stature could bring meaning to her life. Beatings and abuse had taught her well. She knew better now and would never be fooled again.

She glanced at him, enjoying the way his hardened jaw and glittering eyes evinced his determination to see her. He looked at her without flinching, so direct as to be nearly rude, yet there was an honesty behind the look that Catherine found refreshing. It told her Miles, like her, was uninterested in adhering to the restrictions of polite society forbidding forthrightness and candor. He was interested in her and saw no need to pretend otherwise.

"There is a concert tomorrow afternoon in St. James' Park," she said in response. "Perhaps you would care to join me?"

"It has been some time since I last attended a concert."

When he did not elaborate, Catherine allowed a teasing smile to curve her lips. "Shall I guess as to whether you would care to attend this one?"

"Of course not." He smiled back. "I shall call for you with my carriage."

"I take myself," Catherine countered, shaking her head. "The concert begins at three, so I will look for you there an hour before." She would not waver on that point.

He acquiesced with a brief nod. "Very well."

How refreshing that he didn't push for her reasons why. Clearly Miles was a man who understood secrets and presumed she had her reasons for keeping them.

He grasped her fingers for the last time that evening and raised her hand to his lips. "Until tomorrow."

He turned her hand over and brushed a soft kiss against her palm, sweeping just the barest hint of his tongue against her sensitive skin as he did so.

Catherine inhaled a sharp breath over the unexpected, erotic touch, but just as quickly as Miles had lifted her hand he let it go, leaving behind promises of more to come.

She watched him walk back inside, choosing to remain behind for a few minutes longer. The rain would begin falling at any moment, but for the time being, Catherine closed her eyes and allowed the wind to swirl around her. How fortuitous to have met Miles on the very day she'd parted ways with George. She could not have planned better had destiny itself intervened. Already she looked forward to the concert tomorrow.

Catherine breathed in the charged air and opened her eyes as she exhaled, noticing the slight quickening of her heart at the mere thought of being with Miles again. But then, for a brief moment, she questioned the force of her reaction. It was highly uncharacteristic and made her wonder whether seeing him again was a course best not followed.

She dismissed that idea as quickly as it came. She'd resolved never to become emotionally attached to another man, but physical passion was hers to explore to its fullest extent. And for however long their mutual interest in one another stayed alive, the days ahead were sure to be pleasurable indeed.

Chapter Three

The maid lifted the top of the ribboned box and exhaled a sigh of pleasure as she gazed upon the contents inside.

"'Tis the most beautiful I have ever seen," she announced, carefully drawing Catherine's new lace hat out of the box as though the slightest bump would shatter it to pieces. "And I know just how to style your hair so you may show it off."

Catherine laughed and shook a finger at her maid. "Try to restrain yourself, Hannah. Despite fashion, I do not want the height of my hair rivaling Pisa's leaning tower. Let us strive for something a bit more sedate, shall we?"

"Yes, miss. As you wish."

The girl went to work on Catherine's dark locks, curling tresses to frame her face and hang down her back. Once Hannah was finished, she bobbed a quick curtsy and left the room. Catherine completed her morning ritual by touching dabs of scent behind her ears and at her throat. With a final glance in her looking glass, she left to go down to the breakfast room.

As she sat at the small table, eating a poached egg and bread lathered with butter and marmalade, Hannah came forward with a note atop a silver salver.

"This came just now, Miss Sheffield." She held the salver so Catherine could take the note.

She recognized the handwriting at once, and smiled. "Thank you, Hannah," she said, dismissing the maid. She broke the wax seal and laid open the note, written on elegant and expensive parchment. It was from Audrey.

My dear,

It has been some time since I saw you last, and I hope this missive finds you in high spirits. Do come next week Thursday for dinner. I have invited a small gathering, some of whom you know, others who are sure to become enamored of you on sight. We are certain to have a festive evening. Until then, be well.

Yours, Audrey

With surprise, Catherine realized Audrey was correct—it had been well over two weeks since Catherine had last seen her dear friend. She signaled for notepaper and dashed off a reply, accepting her invitation and promising to pay a call the next day. After Catherine had sealed the letter, she sat back in her chair, sipping watered ale and thinking of Audrey.

In the six years since she'd met her, Audrey had become the best friend Catherine had ever known, and she knew their relationship would last a lifetime. In a way it was ironic, since the circumstances surrounding her most meaningful acquaintance had been the most horrendous period of Catherine's life.

Audrey was of the opinion that even in the worst of situations something fortunate always occurs. At the time, mired in the midst of personal hell, Catherine had refused to believe it. But now, with the passage of time and the clarity of hindsight, she'd begun to think perhaps Audrey was right.

Through her marriage to Robert Siddon, the Earl of

Sheffield, Audrey was a distant relation of Catherine's former husband, John Underhill. When her beloved Earl of Sheffield passed away, leaving Audrey a fortune, she did not sit around forever in idle despair. She mourned her husband for the proper period of time and then began to live her own life.

She promptly moved out of their well-appointed but somewhat small London town home into a well-appointed and sprawling estate outside the city's center. Although the cultured art and refined decoration of the house was without flaw, Audrey's move was considered eccentric by some, outrageous by others, and was not approved of by any of the "friends" with whom Audrey and the earl were acquainted. The free-spirited Lady Sheffield was only too happy to cut her ties with them. In her not-so-humble opinion, they were entirely unsuitable for the independent woman she had become.

Despite Audrey and the earl having been childless, Audrey still maintained relations with both her family and his, respecting the blood ties forever binding people together. It was because of that determination to keep in touch with family that Audrey and Catherine had met, and their friendship had been sealed from that very first day. Audrey, in fact, had designated Catherine as the sole inheritor of her estate.

Catherine finished the last of her bread and sat back in her chair, her eyes narrowing with anger whenever she was violated by thoughts of her brutish husband. One memory in particular was a frequent visitor. She and John were scheduled to attend a party of Audrey's, and it was to be the first time Catherine would meet her. But when the day of the party arrived

John had been in one of his moods, and it took but a single, inconsequential incident for his hand to go flying against Catherine's cheek. At that point they had been married for less than a month, and it was the first time he'd been violent toward her.

At first, because Catherine had been so young and gullible, she'd actually thought John's anger was her fault and his punishment was just. She had, after all, forgotten he did not care for creamed peas.

"Why was that offal on my table," he'd bellowed. Hadn't he told her once before of his dislike for it?

Catherine wasn't certain, surely he must have, but she did not remember and as a result had failed to adhere to his wishes. John decided she needed a reminder never to repeat that mistake, and a back-handed slap had done nicely.

Catherine had been too shocked to cry, too convinced of her failure to protest. Instead she apologized, again and again, and when John allowed her to pleasure him in bed to make up for her error, Catherine was determined to do better. Her patronizing lout of a husband had agreed to give his "silly little wife" another chance, and her naïve young self had been eternally grateful.

They attended the party that evening, although the mark of John's slap still darkened her cheek. Audrey had noticed at once. Even while introductions were being made her eyes blazed with fury when she looked upon the bruise. No sooner had they joined the other guests when Audrey pulled Catherine aside and insisted she come along to see Audrey's collection of antique vases.

The two of them—one just barely a woman, the

other wizened beyond her years—entered a small room away from the party where Audrey proceeded to inform Catherine she was not to put up with John's abuse. Audrey explained she knew John through her late husband and was aware of his violent nature. It was something John's family attempted to keep hidden; indeed, it was the very reason Catherine's marriage to him had easily been arranged.

Though her own family was untitled and had little coin, their reputation—clean and pure as a newborn babe's—was priceless. The wealthy landowning Underhills seized the opportunity to scour their family name by linking their black sheep son with an innocent girl whose background was flawless.

Catherine's family had known nothing of John's sordid ways and his habit of taking aggressions out on women, and Catherine could never bring herself to reveal the truth. Besides, it mattered not to her family. Marriage was an arrangement for life. Any other option would never be considered.

It was only unconventional Audrey who warned Catherine to get away, though to no surprise Catherine hadn't yet possessed the courage to do so. It had regrettably taken two more years before she would follow the older woman's advice and escape.

But in those two years, the women's friendship had deepened. When Catherine finally made her late-night dash from John's home and from his brother, Simon, it had been to Audrey where she'd found freedom and the courage to begin a new life.

"More ale, miss?"

The quiet voice of her maid shook Catherine from her reverie.

"Thank you, Hannah, no. I have some correspondence to attend to and then shall be leaving around two o'clock. If you could ensure my hat has been brushed prior to my departure that shall be all."

"Very good."

While the maid rushed off to do her bidding, Catherine wiped her mouth and rose from the table. It was time to focus on more pleasant topics, and Miles Hawkins easily fit that description. In fact, the mere thought of him quickened her heart. Strange, that.

What was it about him? She had met and enjoyed the pleasures of several handsome men, so it couldn't be only his striking looks that intrigued her so. Perhaps it was his apparent disdain for conformity that drew her to him. She, after all, was one of the most unconventional women she knew, and kindred spirits were difficult to find. Audrey was one of them. Catherine wondered, with surprising hope, if Miles would be as well.

When the hour of departure arrived and she stepped outdoors, she was greeted with warm and sunny weather, a faint breeze stirring the air. The trees and flowers exploded with vibrant color, yesterday's rain having washed away the normal dirt and dust. Catherine noticed as she rode in her carriage that even the streets of London seemed cleaner than usual, although it would change as the day wore on and the city teemed with the hustle and grime of life.

As she neared the periphery of St. James' Park, the din of street vendors and cacophony from the marketplaces were replaced by the faint strains of violins as the players warmed up for the concert. Catherine alighted from her carriage and entered the park on foot, already anticipating the afternoon of music.

She looked around at the gathered crowd, seeking Miles. She found him standing among the mingling guests, resplendent and virile in his dark satin blue frock coat and plush breeches. When his searing gaze met with hers, the heat of a blush scorched her cheeks.

"Miss Sheffield." He nodded a greeting as he approached, maintaining a respectable distance between them. He took her fingers in his and brushed a chaste kiss across her hand.

The burn of his lips from that barest contact evoked memories of his fingertips brushing the sides of her breast. Butterflies in her stomach took flight. "A pleasure to see you again, Lord Miles."

"I can assure you, the pleasure is mine." He kept his voice low, as if whispering intimacies for her ears only.

Pulses of arousal fluttered between her legs. Her breath hitched in her throat. She looked away for a moment, needing to collect herself. His raw masculinity engulfed her, flooding with her such desire it rendered her senseless. Heavens above, she was reacting like a virgin bride about to be deflowered. She breathed in, a deep calming breath that centered her and returned her control.

Turning back toward him, she replied, "Then it shall be an afternoon to savor for us both."

As she took his arm while they made their way to the seats set up front, his chiseled muscles flexed beneath the fine-cut sleeve of his coat. Not wanting to appear rude, she surreptitiously glanced at Miles' clothing.

It was all finely made of expensive material, yet there was a casualness in his manner of dress and lack of wig that defied fussiness of any kind. She remembered how he had appeared last evening before they'd departed for the balcony, bored and underwhelmed by the opulence of the ball, as though he'd been in that situation a hundred times before.

Undoubtedly he was a man of wealth, but who was his family? His name was not one she knew, although there were so many people in London it was impossible to be acquainted with them all. She realized that aside from his name and the heated passion of his kiss, Catherine knew nothing of the man she'd already determined would be her next lover. With eager anticipation, she looked forward to learning more.

"Where shall we sit?" She gestured toward the seats.

"I leave the choice up to you."

"Then I hope you will not mind that we sit up front." She walked swiftly forward, pleased by how easily he'd conceded to her request.

As they took their seats, she continued, "I like to see the musicians as well as hear them. I find it fascinating to watch the talent of the players. The way they produce such beautiful sounds from wood and horsetail hairs is nothing short of a miracle. As though the voices of angels are hidden inside the instruments."

She flushed with excitement as she awaited the start of the music. The invitation for Miles to accompany her was not simply an idyllic way to spend the remainder of the afternoon. Music was important to her, and she hoped he would share her delight.

The hour approached, and more and more guests

began taking their seats. A fashionably dressed older couple strolled by, the height of the woman's hat like a tower atop her head. When she caught sight of Miles, she halted.

"Lord Miles." A warm smile touched her lips, yet the woman's eyes registered faint surprise. "How good to see you."

Miles stood and took the woman's hand. "And you as well, Lady Wilton." He nodded toward the gentleman by her side. "Lord Wilton."

The other man returned the greeting. "It's a pleasure to see you out, Hawkins."

Miles swiftly turned and introduced Catherine.

The couple returned a warm greeting before continuing on, and Catherine and Miles sat back down. The exchange had been nothing but pleasant, yet Catherine sensed all three were aware of something she was not. She wondered at it, but then set her curiosity aside, reminding herself it was best to maintain emotional distance with her lovers.

As the first notes of the concert took wing, Catherine closed her eyes and surrendered herself to the music. She allowed it to overtake her completely, to infuse the space around her with its sweetness. She had not heard the afternoon's piece before, noted in the program as a violin concerto in D major by the modern composer Mozart. Its simplistic beauty swept her away.

When the music ended, she turned to Miles, wanting to ask if he'd enjoyed the performance. But the question died on her tongue the moment she glanced over. Miles' focus was squarely on her.

Their eyes met and held, a spark of desire igniting the air. For the first time in Catherine's life, any thoughts she may have had about what would next be performed were swept away like dust in a storm.

Instead, she luxuriated in Miles' sheer male magnetism. He exuded sensuality the way a hearth fire emits heat, seducing her with his eyes. His mere look alone stripped her naked. Her hands trembled where she held them, modestly folded in her lap. Her pulse spiked. She shivered with mounting need as a low throb quickened in her core.

At last, as the opening notes of the second piece filled the space around them, she finally tore away her gaze and broke the connection. Silently, she expelled a calming breath, stunned by how Miles had so easily diverted her attention from the music. Such a thing had never happened before.

As always, the performance ended far too soon. Catherine was forever perplexed why concert-goers could never manage more than an hour and a quarter of music when she could spend the entire afternoon and still want more. Yet, as always, the last notes faded after the conventional amount of time and guests swiftly rose from their chairs. Miles took Catherine's hand, leading her over to where refreshments were sold.

After handing her a lemon ice, they made their way to stand beneath a leafy tree where they could talk in relative privacy and escape the day's heat.

"Did you enjoy it?" she asked.

"The music?"

Catherine laughed. "Of course, the music. What else?"

He took a long sip of his ale and wiped away beads of sweat from his brow. "The music was certainly pleasant enough," he said at last. "But there have been a great many things I've enjoyed in the park this afternoon. The sunshine, this ale," he nodded at the drink, and then his voice dipped down, "but in particular, the company."

Her pulse quickened at his tantalizing response. "I am glad the concert pleased you."

"You seemed quite taken by it yourself."

"As I am with almost all music," she affirmed. "The composer Mozart has especially captured my interest. Some say the music is too spirited, but I find it beautiful."

"Indeed it is."

She spooned the lemon ice and let it melt on her tongue. "Anyway, who is to say what accounts for one's preference? I would not doubt there are some who'd deem the chanting of ancient monks overly spirited."

Miles laughed. "You have no fear of expressing your opinion."

"I do not, no. Particularly in the appropriate company."

He seemed to recognize the compliment. "You flatter me."

"Actually it is you who flatters me. Men and women alike often disapprove of females speaking their mind."

"In which case they are fools."

With each passing moment, he intrigued her more and more. It was rare, indeed, to find a man who welcomed intellectual conversation with a woman. Throwing aside her customary caution, Catherine wanted, suddenly, to know absolutely everything about Lord Miles Hawkins. What else did he like? What did he dislike? Who was his family?

She turned her head toward him, questions nearly bursting from her lips. "Where did you—"

"Hawkins!" An expensively tailored man sporting a tri-cornered hat and walking stick approached them, arm outstretched. He clapped Miles on the back as they shook hands. "I haven't seen you in over two years," he exclaimed, surprise evident in his voice, "although I'd heard you've re-entered the scene. 'Tis good to have you back."

Miles nodded once, his expression instantly tight. "Thank you, Edmund."

Edmund seemed oblivious to Miles' discomfort. "Nasty business that all was, Hawkins," he said, shaking his head. "I couldn't even imagine it. Must have been hell—pure hell."

Miles did not respond, but the newcomer chatted on undeterred. "You seem to have recovered well enough. And as I said, 'tis good to have you back." He turned toward Catherine. "Good day, fair lady. I am Sir Edmund Budding."

"Good day to you, Sir Edmund," Catherine replied. "Catherine Sheffield."

Edmund bowed and lifted his hat, revealing a tuft of grey hair peeking out from beneath his wig. He took her outstretched hand and brushed a kiss across the back of it, holding it longer than he should have. "It is a pleasure, Miss Sheffield."

Catherine withdrew her hand with slight force, showing Edmund Budding what she thought of his manners. She turned to Miles. "Have you and Sir Edmund known each other long?"

"Not at all," Miles was quick to reply, as if

prohibiting Edmund from saying otherwise. "We are acquainted through Tom's coffeehouse."

"Indeed," Edmund vigorously agreed, apparently not in the least put off by Miles' cool reception. "Hawkins is a great reader of the daily newsletters, and the other fellows and I would frequent the coffeehouse to see if we could get him to tell us what goes on in the rest of the world!" He emitted a hearty laugh as if he'd just told a great joke.

Miles' strained smile failed to reach his eyes. He swallowed twice in quick succession and held his posture stiffly erect, as if preparing to ward off blows.

Sir Edmund, apparently blind to Miles' discomfort, launched into a lengthy description of a dinner party he'd just attended. "And then the dreadful fish course began, and I—"

"It has been a pleasure, Sir Edmund." Catherine paid no mind to interrupting his tiresome monologue. "But it is with regret we must leave you. I have a pressing engagement I must attend, and Lord Miles has kindly offered to ensure I am escorted home safely. Good day, sir."

"Nice seeing you, Edmund," Miles added, taking the cue as he clapped Budding on the back. Catherine took Miles' proffered arm.

They strolled in silence for several moments until they reached the periphery of the park. The distant location and late day hour likely explained the paucity of other people. The profuse trees lent the area a feeling more forest than park.

They walked into the dense thicket and were rewarded with an atmosphere cool and hushed, like that of a church, without anyone else around. They stopped beneath a leafy tree, but Miles' levity from earlier in the day had vanished. Tightness around his lips and the stark, drawn expression on his face left him looking like a man haunted by the weighty burden of grief.

She recalled what Budding had said. *Must have been hell—pure hell.* Her eyes welled with sympathy. She didn't know what tortured Miles, but the reasons didn't matter. Whatever they were, she understood his pain.

He looked over, meeting her gaze, and took in a breath. "You may be wondering—"

"No, Miles." She shook her head. "What you choose to share with me about yourself—or not share—will be your decision alone and done in your own time. Until then, you need not say a thing."

He cleared his throat and she noticed his hands ball into fists. "'Tis difficult to find the right words."

"Which is why you needn't find them with me."

He took a step closer, looking into her eyes. "You are an uncommon woman, Catherine Sheffield."

"Yes."

He smiled. "And quite agreeable."

"When it suits me."

Miles leaned into his right arm, resting against the tree. His despair of moments ago faded, leaving in its wake the spark of desire. He lifted his left hand and trailed his fingers across her cheek. "And does this suit you?"

He bent closer so they were inches apart, the warm exhalations of his breath gliding across his face. With his forefinger he caressed her top lip and then bottom, circling her mouth with a touch as light as air. He inserted just the tip of his finger into her mouth, sweeping it across her tongue, then withdrawing it to paint the moisture across her bottom lip.

"It does." Her response was little more than a whisper. The excited beats of her pulse trembled like leaves stirred by the wind.

"How about this?" he asked, his hand straying downward to trace light, sensual patterns along her throat. When he reached the indentation at the base of her neck he paused, stroking her collarbone. Then he dipped lower, teasing the swell of her bosom before sliding his palm over her left breast, caressing it through the fabric of her dress.

Her nipple puckered in response to his touch. Slow, delicious pulses throbbed low in her groin. Her eyes drifted closed, lost in a carnal haze.

"Look at me." He lightly pinched her nipple. "I want to watch you get aroused."

"How do you know I will?" she challenged, though the breathiness of her reply betrayed her bravado.

"Trust me, you will." The flat of his hand glided over her belly, drawing ever closer to the apex of her legs. "I'm about to make it so. You shall feel my touch all over your body, and I shall hear you moan."

Although the park was empty of visitors, Miles stepped even closer to Catherine to ensure his body shielded hers. Then with one hand he lifted her skirt and chemise while he slid the other beneath the silk material to caress her thighs. Where his fingertips stroked, a line of fire sizzled along her skin.

Her breath whooshed from her lungs. Her heartbeat soared. Miles' hand roamed upward from her thigh to cup her mons then he brazenly slid a finger through the soaking folds of her pussy and lightly stroked her throbbing clit.

She gasped, shocked yet thrilled at his daring. Taking her cue from his boldness, she spread her legs farther apart, needing more of his skilled caresses to soothe her burning ache. He smiled as though she'd given him a reward and continued his assault. Her blood roared in her ears, skin burning from Miles' attention. Her breaths came hot and quick.

"Let go, Catherine," he whispered, increasing the pressure of his hand. "Let me see your desire. I would know how far I can take you."

It was as though he were testing her, seeing if he could expose her limitations. She rose to the challenge and nodded. "If you dare."

"Oh," he growled beneath his breath. "I dare."

In the back of her mind she knew the risk they took, sharing passion outdoors in which any given moment might expose them to prying eyes. But it was an experience she'd never had, and the danger added an element of sensuality far too delicious to resist. She rested against the tree and ever so slightly arched her back to meet the pressure of Miles' hand. She lifted her arm and placed it around his neck.

To her surprise, he shook his head and withdrew his hand from beneath her skirt. Reaching behind his head, he unwound her arm and settled it by her side. "Not this time," he said. "Now is for you alone. I can touch you, but you must not touch me."

"But—"

"If you can stand it." His eyes gleamed as he teased, provoking her in a way she'd never known.

With the tip of his tongue he licked her lips, holding off on fully kissing her. Instead, he tugged at the silk scarf loosely tied about her neck, easily removing the fabric and exposing the swell of her breasts above the gown's plunging neckline. Then he lightly pulled down on the gown enough to be able to dip his hand beneath the neckline and withdraw her bare breast.

Catherine hissed in a sharp breath of air from the searing heat of Miles' touch. Her nipple hardened like the pit of a cherry as he rolled it between his fingers. She longed to wrap her arms around him, drawing him into her embrace, and his refusal to allow her to do so heightened her arousal until just as promised, she moaned aloud.

She cast her gaze downward between their bodies. The bulge of Miles' cock thrust against his breeches. Beads of sweat clung to his temples and she knew he burned for release. But his satisfaction this time seemed to be from pleasuring her and she accepted his wish. Next time she would be the one giving pleasure.

He bent down to dot kisses along her neckline and the swell of her breast. Flames of desire consumed her. "Oooh!"

He looked up, eyes glittering. "Shall I stop?"

"Never."

"As you wish." A faint smile touched his lips before he resumed his work.

With excruciating slowness, his tongue painted a scorching wet trail around her breast. Blood roared in her ears and her heart pounded so fiercely she wondered if Miles could feel the thumping beneath his lips. It mattered not. Her head swam from his sensual assault. He teased her to the brink of madness, flicking at her nipple with his tongue but not sucking it.

"Please," she begged, her voice like a whimper.

He lifted his head. "Patience, Miss Sheffield."

"It's gone missing." She thrust her chest forward, demanding attention, but still he held off. Catherine thought she would go mad from Miles' torment, frustration mounting by not being allowed to touch him.

Around and around he kissed until, at last, he took her hardened nipple into his mouth, swirling his tongue over the sensitized skin, grazing it ever so lightly with his teeth. Her hands gripped the rough bark of the tree she leaned against while Miles' tortuous expertise with his lips and tongue shot fire to her throbbing core. Moisture trickled down her thighs as her hips swayed.

Release danced within her grasp as Miles continued to suck her sensitive nipples. Yet she craved more, just a little. Her eyes closed as she panted with unfulfilled need. If only he would lift her skirts once again…

A warm breeze fluttered loose strands of her hair, a brief reminder of their outdoor locale. Yet with Miles standing directly before her, his large muscular frame serving as shield from prying eyes, they were cloaked in relative secrecy. Even so, Catherine gave thanks for the isolation in that area of the park.

She allowed her head to fall back against the tree, indulging in Miles' caresses as she would a luxurious bath. After a time his kisses once more slid tantalizingly along her throat, then they brushed her cheeks, her forehead, until at last he claimed her lips.

His torrid kiss was like an explosion of fire. Catherine opened her mouth to Miles, returning his kiss with frenzied passion. She dipped her tongue into the hot recesses of his mouth, tasting him, breathing him in as if he'd become a part of her. He groaned low in ecstasy as she pulled away and kissed his throat, licking the heated, salty skin, then returned once more to continue kissing his mouth. Now it was her turn to groan aloud as Miles' hand crept downward once more to cup between her legs.

She breathed into his mouth as his fingers stroked her sensitive clit through the material of her dress. She wantonly pressed herself against the palm of his hand, already panting from his earlier teases and desperate for release. But Miles held back, pulling away as she strained forward, causing her to nearly cry aloud in frustration while continuing to stoke the fires of her lust.

He gave a swift look around, ensuring they were still alone. Then he bent forward and, using both hands, grasped the voluminous layers of petticoats, chemise, and the gown itself and edged up the skirts, bunching them at her waist. Holding them against her body with his hand, he raised his face so his gaze burned directly into her eyes.

"Wrap your leg around me."

Her mouth went dry. She licked nervously at her lips, her heart slamming against her ribcage. For one wild moment she wondered if he issued his command in jest, but a single look in his lust-black eyes revealed the truth. He would pleasure here, outdoors, and she would let him.

She lifted her thigh and placed it around his waist.

"Beautiful," he whispered as he slid his fingers along her calf. Then he aimed higher, gliding over her knee and the smooth, heated surface of her inner thigh, inching ever closer to her sex. At last he brushed her slick outer folds until finally sinking two fingers into her pulsing wet pussy.

Catherine gasped, aching with need, almost fearful Miles would not continue. But to her vast relief he did not deny her but instead continued thrusting again and again, just where she needed it, picking up speed as her arousal increased. At the same time he made certain the base of his hand rhythmically slapped her needy clit, the frenzied strokes making her cry out shamelessly and shoot her hips forward to drive his fingers deeper inside her.

He returned his kisses to her breasts, bathing them with attention, bringing her ever closer to spiraling out of control. The pleasure he gave her was unlike anything she'd ever had. Being unable to touch him meant every moment centered around her needs and desires, far beyond her most wicked fantasies.

She was close, so close. Her eyes drifted shut, and she rested her head against the tree, trusting him to do as he wished. Heat surrounded her, burning, licks of flame throbbing deep in her as she strained to douse them with release.

The still air was heavy with her musky scent and the slaps of Miles' hand as he ground against her. Her lips parted, and she moaned aloud, climax mere seconds from her grasp. Pressure built, ready to explode. Fluttering pulses intensified, turned to throbs. Her hips rocked back and forth, her walls deliciously stretching against Miles' thrusting fingers. At last her entire body trembled, and she cried out, her breasts heaving as she shuddered with release.

When her breathing began to slow, he discreetly pulled away, helping her straighten her garments and retrieving the silk scarf that had fallen to the ground.

She tied it around her neck and smoothed her hair, giving Miles a coy smile. "That was a most unexpected pleasure."

With the dark haze of lust still staining his eyes, Miles held his hand to his nose and breathed in her scent, closing his eyes as if inhaling the exotic aroma of a rare perfume.

Then he looked back at her, a faint smile touching his lips. "For me as well." He held out his arm as they began walking back toward their respective carriages.

The forlorn call of a mourning dove filled the air around them as they re-entered the nearly deserted park. A scant few couples strolled about, heads bowed low as they chatted. Miles stopped for a moment and turned to face Catherine.

"When I said earlier that you are uncommon I meant it in the best possible way. You are like no woman I've met before. There's a connection between us; I know you feel it as well. This was something I wanted to do, and I'm pleased you allowed it."

She smiled at him, her skin tingling with the afterglow of passion. "'Twas not a difficult decision. Yet pleasurable though it was, I still prefer when intimacy is shared. Next time will not be mine alone to enjoy."

As she'd hoped, the promise of a future encounter seemed to stir him. He said nothing in response, but lifted a hand, fingers extended, to reach behind her back and bring her forward, pressing her body against his. He leaned into her, placing his lips upon her neck and nipping at the skin, tiny bite marks claiming her as his.

"Believe me, Miss Sheffield," he murmured

against her throat, "the pleasure was not yours alone."

She gasped as his hand slipped between their bodies to palm her breast, smoothing over the fabric to circle against the nipple and make it harden to stone. His outrageous boldness excited her as no one before. Moisture pooled as her pussy throbbed with hot pulses of need. This was madness. She took a step back.

"Show me more," she said, looking into his ink black eyes, "when opportunity next presents itself."

His hand dropped away, and he gave her a nod of understanding. They resumed their walk in comfortable silence, having just shared something unique certain to stay with them forever.

When they reached the area where they would part, Catherine said, "Thank you, Lord Miles. I have had an extraordinary day."

"As have I." He brushed a kiss against her lips. "But I must see you again."

"When?"

"Tomorrow. Come for dinner to my home in Kensington. At eight."

It was soon, so soon, three days in a row. Catherine typically kept her suitors more at bay, ever careful that emotions not get entangled in the physical pleasure. But it was impossible to resist him.

"Eight o'clock," she agreed, anticipation building already.

He assisted her into her carriage, and with a final parting nod turned and walked away. Catherine signaled the driver and then settled back for the short ride to her own home.

She had not been exaggerating to Miles when she'd described the afternoon as extraordinary. Allowing him to pleasure her as he had—outdoors, with the risk of discovery—was beyond anything she'd ever experienced. Yet there was something so intensely different about Miles that she wanted to go where he took her, wherever it may be. She eagerly awaited the journey ahead.

Chapter Four

"You've taken a new lover," Audrey pronounced.

Catherine laughed as they enjoyed the afternoon on the back terrace of Audrey's magnificent home. "I have not. Not exactly, anyway."

Audrey plucked grapes from a bowl on the table and studied Catherine as she nibbled them. "The flush on your cheeks and sparkle in your eyes are not caused from fever, and 'tis summer so the cold hasn't contributed, either. That can mean only one thing—you've taken a new lover or are on the verge of doing so."

Catherine's mind flashed back to yesterday's sensual tryst in the park. No surprise her cheeks were flushed. Some may not have noticed, but Audrey's sharp gaze missed nothing, especially where Catherine was concerned. Not that Catherine would want to hide anything from her friend. In fact, she surprised herself with her eagerness to tell Audrey about Miles.

"I did meet someone recently," she acknowledged, reaching for her wine glass.

"Anyone I know?"

Catherine shook her head. "I am not familiar with the name, though perhaps you are. "'Tis Lord Miles Hawkins."

"Hawkins? Of the Belthorpe estate in Newbury?"

"I do not know. We have not discussed his family."

Audrey looked thoughtful. "If we are speaking of the same Hawkins, then the father is James Hawkins, the Marquis of Newbury, and the first born is Richard. Old wealth, a lot of it, and the grace to be quiet about it."

"The man I met must be a second son then, unless we speak of two different families."

"'Tis a possibility, although unlikely there are two unrelated Hawkins families with that kind of money."

"True." Catherine sipped her wine and settled into her chair as she prepared to tell Audrey about Miles. In addition to the wine, the servants had brought them a variety of fruits—grapes, figs, raspberries, and quinces—and a bowl of sweetened cream.

"Whatever the case," Catherine began, "we met at the Kenworth ball on Saturday."

"He has captured your interest so soon?"

"He has, yes."

Audrey's brows furrowed for a moment. "I thought you were entertaining the Earl of Clifton?"

"No longer."

"And you are interested in Hawkins already." She stated that last as a fact rather than a question.

A starling landed on the ground near Catherine's feet and cast a hopeful glance her way. She smiled and tossed down some blueberries, taking a moment to consider her response before speaking aloud to Audrey. "I trust you do not disapprove that my interest in someone new has piqued so quickly?"

"Disapprove?" The surprise on Audrey's face was almost comical. "Catherine, love, you know me better than that. I of all people applaud your decision never to marry again."

"'Tis a difficult course to follow."

"Difficult does not begin to describe it. I warned you of it."

"And I am ever grateful."

"You must endure the judgment of others who are too narrow-minded and fearful to question what is expected. But you are like me, Catherine. An independent, passionate woman who dares to live without the sole objective of snaring a husband. I had a good marriage the first time around but even so am not inclined to become a wife ever again. But after what you went through with John..."

It was not necessary for Audrey to finish. They both knew all too well the horror of Catherine's one and only marriage.

"Well." Catherine changed directions toward a topic more pleasant. "That's just it, is it not? I had a horrid experience being married and none of the sensual delights I had heard so much about. It seemed unfair I did not even get to experience that."

Audrey smiled. "No longer."

"No indeed." She threw another handful of blueberries to the starling. "I shall never again allow the vile misuse of my emotions, but exploring the physical elements of love is a delectable pursuit."

"One I have enjoyed for years." Audrey raised her glass to Catherine in a show of solidarity. "And damn anyone to hell who disapproves." After taking a healthy swallow, she settled back in her chair. "So tell me about your latest conquest."

Oddly enough, Audrey's off-handed remark diminishing Miles to simply a "conquest" settled badly with Catherine, like sour milk curdling in the stomach.

But she shook away the thought as quickly as it had come. She took lovers for lovemaking and nothing more.

"To begin with, he is dashing in the extreme."

"I should expect nothing less."

"Very tall. His height even makes me feel small."

Audrey clicked her tongue. "Never belittle your graceful stature, Catherine. You are like an elegant willow tree, tall yet lithesome."

"You always know how to make me feel beautiful." Catherine's compliment was not given lightly. Given what Audrey had done for her, she felt a bond closer to her than she did her own mother. And in many ways, the bond they shared was thicker than blood.

"What else?" Audrey's curiosity was endless.

"His skin is bronzed, the most becoming shade of copper I have ever laid eyes on, and his hair and eyes are dark as well."

"How delicious."

Catherine laughed. "He's also strong, more than I would have expected, based on the elegant clothing."

"You mean 'tis possible he does more than sit around smoking pipes and drinking brandy every day?" Her voice was laced with a touch of disapproval at the common habit of much of London's nobles.

"'Twould seem so, though I know not what."

"Whatever it is, let us hope he continues."

"Agreed." Catherine picked up her glass and tilted it with a nod of approval to Audrey. She took a long sip, enjoying the warm blush sliding through her veins as she drank. Her finger traced the rim of the goblet and she looked over the edge of the glass at her friend.

"I am seeing him again. Tonight."

As Catherine assumed, Audrey immediately picked up the thread of her thoughts. "When did you see him last?"

"Yesterday, at the concert in St. James'."

"And before that?"

"The evening prior. 'Twas when I met him." Catherine almost winced; she knew what was coming.

"Three days in a row? You know it is not a wise idea, particularly when you do not wish to become emotionally entangled."

"I know, I know. But I am so..." She shrugged, unable to find exactly the right word. "So excited by him. He is impossible to resist."

"Like a fine dessert."

They both laughed over their shared weakness of sweets. But once the amusement passed, Audrey leaned in toward Catherine, eyeing her with a serious face.

"You must take caution, my dear. Emotions can easily take root when physical excitement is high. Clearly Hawkins has captured your interest."

"You need not concern yourself, Audrey," Catherine insisted. "We shall see each other for a period of time to our mutual liking, and when the interest wanes I shall end it. Like always."

"He may not be agreeable."

"That matters not." Catherine shook her head. "It never has with your affairs, and it never does with mine. I will not risk emotional involvement, and I know exactly how to prevent it."

"If he is in fact a second son, he is likely not feeling the pressure to secure a bride."

"Perhaps not. We did not discuss it."

"You surprise me." Audrey reached for the fruit bowl and scooped some melon onto a small plate in front of her. "Generally you are more familiar with the men you choose than you are with Hawkins. Did he share nothing of himself with you?"

Catherine tossed aside Audrey's question. "His background is of no concern. After all, he knows nothing of mine."

"Nor will he. Ever."

The cold finality in Audrey's voice revealed her love for Catherine more overtly than words of endearment ever could. Catherine's heart went immediately soft as she reflected on all Audrey had done for her. On impulse, she leaned over and gave her friend a hug.

"For everything," she responded to the question in Audrey's eyes. "For rescuing me from John, for hiding me from Simon. For teaching me what it means to be a true friend. For transforming and saving my life."

"Anyone would have done the same," Audrey insisted.

"'Tis not so. When Lucy Underhill raced through the night four years ago to escape the wrath of her husband's brother, there was no one in the world to turn to but you. Where else could I have possibly gone?"

Since the time of Catherine's marriage both her parents had passed and she had no other family. In any case, had they lived, they would have insisted her duty was to face Simon and not scurry away like a frightened rat. The reputation of the family was at stake. Doing anything else was unthinkable.

"It does not matter. Lucy Underhill no longer exists. You left her behind the night John died.

Catherine Sheffield is who you are now, and Catherine Sheffield you shall always remain."

"I'm so grateful for all you have done for me, Audrey. Allowing me to use your name and pose as your niece was a brilliant stroke of genius."

"Oh, nonsense." Audrey brushed off the praise, although Catherine knew by the stain on her friend's cheeks that she appreciated the gratitude. "'Twas no stroke of genius. You'd never lived before in London so you were known by no one. Telling everyone you'd been abroad for years until your parents' unexpected passing fit in perfectly with why none of my friends had ever met you. It has all worked out."

Audrey sipped her wine, a thoughtful expression on her face. "Even Simon hasn't a clue of your whereabouts, and 'tis likely he never will. He and John used to journey to London on occasion, but they haven't now for years. The gossips say something sordid happened, though I have never known for certain."

She took figs from the platter and sat back in her chair. "In any case," she continued, "his lands and business are in the country, so 'tis certain there he shall remain."

"Do you ever..." Catherine faltered, not certain she even wanted to know the answer.

"Go on. What is it?"

"I wondered if you thought about Simon now and again. After all, he *is* your family."

"*You* are my family, Catherine. It matters not that Simon Underhill is a distant cousin through marriage. I receive frequent enough communication from the family to help me keep an eye on him. I want to know where he's about in case he ever gets a vague notion to come to London."

"I should have guessed you would be watching out for me. You always have."

"And I always will."

Catherine swirled the wine in her glass, awash in thoughts of the past. Audrey's comment about family touched a melancholic nerve. Since leaving her former self behind and transforming into Catherine Sheffield, she'd rarely paid mind to her other life. It was a piece of herself best left forgotten.

But on occasion, memories of pleasantries from the past surfaced. She thought sometimes of her parents, even more of her one dear childhood friend, Jane Denbigh. Jane was four years younger than Catherine and at times had been more like a little sister than anything else. But despite the age difference, the girls had been fast friends. Catherine had cared deeply for Jane and regretted she could not ever reveal her whereabouts.

Their shadows stretched long across the lush lawn behind Audrey's elegant home. Catherine rose and prepared to leave. "I shall see you next week for dinner."

"Invite him as well. I would love to know who has captured your interest so quickly."

"Perhaps."

Audrey stood as well and gave Catherine a quick peck on the cheek. "As you wish. I know you frequently keep that part of your life separate. But the offer is there."

They strolled inside, and Audrey signaled for the maid to bring Catherine her hat and cape. After waving goodbye from the window of her carriage, Catherine's thoughts returned once more to Miles. She would see him again in a few short hours, and already she looked forward to it with the anticipation of a child about to receive a treat.

Audrey's observation about how little Catherine knew of him mattered not. For now, they would enjoy each other's company and then go their separate ways. It was always like that. Yet for one brief, passing moment, before she pushed it aside, Catherine sensed the void in her life that Miles' absence would create.

****

The elegant grandeur of the red brick home on fashionable Brook Street in Mayfair far exceeded Catherine's expectation. It was not ostentatiously large, but the tasteful décor both inside and out subtly revealed the owner's wealth.

After passing through the octagonal foyer perfumed with oversized vases of tuberose, Catherine's heels clicked against mosaic patterns of parquet as she followed the staid butler who had greeted her at the door. They drifted past wall hangings, an ornately carved walnut side table flanked by chairs covered in silk damask, and a dignified oil portrait of Miles with a slightly older young man and a younger girl, presumably his siblings.

Though it was against her better judgment, Catherine had to admit curiosity about his family. Would he share any details? Certainly she wouldn't ask, but if he chose to do so she would welcome it.

Rather than depositing her in a waiting room as Catherine had expected, the butler instead led her directly to the dining room where Miles awaited.

Miles greeted Catherine warmly by brushing a kiss across her hand before turning toward the butler. "That will be all for the moment, Evans," he said, dismissing him. "We will take the first course at half past the hour."

With a silent nod, the butler departed and closed the door behind him, leaving Catherine and Miles alone in the dining room.

For a moment he said nothing, his gaze lazily roaming wherever it wished, as if absorbing her through the simple act of looking.

She was secretly thrilled with his reaction, having taken more care than usual with her dress, trying then discarding half a dozen gowns before settling on the emerald green silk trimmed in lace. It matched the color of her eyes and made them sparkle like gems. The neckline was cut enticingly low and filled in with a lace scarf tied about her neck. She'd swept her raven hair into a high chignon, accented with small jeweled hairpins. A cascade of ringlets tumbled down her back.

She raised an eyebrow at him and smiled. "Are you simply going to stand there, Lord Miles, or will you give me a proper greeting?"

"Believe me, Miss Sheffield, you do not wish to know how I'd define a 'proper greeting.' At least not here in the dining room."

Catherine's pulse spiked, and her voice became low and throaty. "I beg to differ."

"Then I am forced to prove my point." Miles stood before her, his towering height enhanced even more so by his panther-like prowess. He took a step forward.

Overwhelmed, she took an involuntary step back. His lips curled into a smile as he advanced once more, closing in on his prey. She shivered, the hair on her arms standing at attention, and again shifted backward.

They continued that way, thrust and parry, until her back collided with a paneled wall. He closed in, resting his left arm against the wall, right next to her ear, his rock hard body trapping her. Her breath caught in her throat as the heady scent of ambergris surrounded her.

He tilted her head up with a single finger beneath her chin. Carnal heat permeated the room. Miles bent low, grazing his lips with hers, not quite a kiss but more of a taste, a promise, of things to come. He used both hands to caress her face, placing his palms beneath her chin as he framed her with his fingers, stroking the skin so enticingly that any thoughts she may have had of escape evaporated like steam.

He swept kisses against her cheek and her forehead, across her eyelids. His touch was tender even while he radiated raw, male heat. He bent lower, pushing aside the scarf to focus attention on the slender column of her throat, nipping at the exposed skin, swirling the tip of his tongue in the indentation at the base.

His kisses were gentle, teasing, drawing out her desire. He was agonizingly slow, sprinkling butterfly kisses against her skin, pulling back when she tried forcing him to give her more. She let out a frustrated, breathy moan, and it was as if she'd given him a signal, something he'd been waiting for. He plunged his fingers through her hair and descended upon her lips.

Pins and jeweled combs rained upon the floor. Curled and coiffed tresses tumbled in waves like spilled ink. Yet none of it mattered to Catherine as Miles devastated her with his lips and tongue. With the first sweep of his mouth against hers she thought only of him, of his power, his heart-stopping looks, and his seemingly insatiable hunger for her.

She could feel his lust, sharp as a dagger, honing her own desire until she wanted, in one mad, desperate moment, to fling aside the crystal goblets, porcelain china, and silver candelabra to climb atop the table and demand he take her.

She had never desired a man as fiercely as she did Miles. She craved him as though he'd been denied to her for years, and she was making up for lost time. It was a crazy, illogical feeling since until three days ago they'd never even met. But Catherine could not deny how much she wanted him now.

His mouth was warm, passionate, welcoming. With each sweep of his tongue against hers, a stab of pure lust plummeted straight between her thighs. It was madness to need him this badly only seconds after seeing him, but the truth was irrefutable.

Ever so slowly, with the patience of a saint, he slid his hands downward. The tips of his fingers stroked her face, then her throat.

"Your skin is softer than the silk of your dress," he murmured.

He traveled lower, reaching the delicate collarbone at the base of her neck. He traced around it, then his fingers reached the knot of the lace scarf. In one deft movement, he untied it and swept it away so it floated like a cloud to the floor. With her neck now bared, he focused his mouth and tongue on her skin, kissing and licking her throat.

His hands continued their descent, at last reaching the swell of her breasts. He spanned his palms across them and he grinned as her nipples hardened beneath the gown, as though reaching for his touch. He moved his palms in small circles against her breast, teasing her, inflaming her further still.

Catherine could not hold back a low, throaty moan. She was hovering on the very edge of telling him to forgo dinner and take her here, in the dining room, fast and hard, for as long as he wanted. But the realization that he consumed her to the point of causing control to slip gave her pause, and she pulled away.

His eyes were still half closed, his breathing swift and shallow. His brows knit as she placed distance between them, but then he seemed to understand why she'd ended the kiss. He looked down at her as their ardor mutually cooled.

She gathered herself, once more poised and elegant, infused with the satisfaction of a contented cat. "If that is your idea of a proper greeting, I have much to look forward to."

"*Very* much, I can assure you."

He stepped away and crossed the room to a side table laden with crystal decanters of dark red wine and Venetian glass goblets. His back was partly turned toward her, but Catherine could see him take several steadying breaths, his hands trembling as they rested atop the table. They both needed a moment to regain control.

His hands steady once more, Miles poured wine for them both. He walked back over to Catherine, glass in hand.

"A toast," he proposed as he handed her the wine. "To our new…friendship." His eyebrows lifted as he spoke, his apparent surprise matching Catherine's.

Yet it took only an instant for her to decide that perhaps her relationship with Miles was indeed, to a certain extent, a friendship. "Very well," she agreed, lifting her glass, "to our friendship."

They toasted and drank. As he set his glass back on the table, a droplet of wine lingered on his bottom lip. He swiped it away with the tip of his tongue. Desire, thick as haze, surged through her blood.

He gestured, indicating the chair at the dining table nearest to where Catherine stood. "Please make yourself comfortable. 'Tis time to sup."

The moment she'd settled and Miles took his place beside her, somber footmen entered the room as if on cue, carrying steaming platters of food. The servants placed every dish on the table—savory beef carbonado, venison pasties, oysters, fresh peas, turnips, and assorted cheeses—before departing as quickly and quietly as they'd arrived.

"What does the lady favor?" Miles asked.

"Anything the gentlemen chooses to serve," she replied breathlessly, still smiling from the realization they would be sharing a quiet dinner for two without the usual presence of hovering footmen. The unexpected intimacy already had her pulse racing.

"I must warn you, my cooks are renowned for their skills in the kitchen. You shall not go hungry."

"Have no fear, Lord Miles, I do not intend to go hungry. For anything."

She noted the sharp intake of his breath at her provocative reply, and liquid heat shot through her as desire stirred anew. She wondered how she'd ever be able to get through dinner.

"Very well." His voice grew suggestively low. "Let

us begin with the pasty." He selected a flaky turnover from the platter, but instead of setting it on Catherine's plate, he placed it on his. Keeping his eyes focused on her, he blew on the pasty and steam drifted toward her. When it sufficiently cooled, he picked it up and broke off a bite-sized piece.

"Your pasty, my lady," he said, holding the piece before her lips.

For an instant Catherine frowned, bemused, but then she understood the game. She raised an eyebrow toward him as she leaned forward and took the piece from his fingers and into her mouth.

Miles was right; the food was delicious. Catherine closed her eyes as she savored the seasoned venison as flavors mingled in her mouth. Then she opened her eyes. Miles watched her with studied intensity, as if trying to discern her thoughts from her expression alone. Catherine suspected he was keen to know her reaction to their unorthodox dinner, from the lack of footmen to his hand-feeding her venison pie. But rather than tell him, she decided to show him.

The beef carbonado sat by her left side, sliced atop the platter and coated with rich gravy. Without hesitation, Catherine selected one of the pieces. She tore a morsel from it and held it before Miles' lips.

"Please, my lord, enjoy. I should not want you to go hungry."

As Catherine had done moments earlier, Miles took the bite she offered, brushing her fingers with the searing heat of his soft lips. He studied her as he slowly ate, as if trying to guess her thoughts.

"Are you enjoying the dish?" She heard the light tremble in her voice.

He nodded. "I am. But I'm enjoying you far more."

He began preparing the next bite for her, but Catherine held out her fingers. A few drops of the carbonado sauce still clung to them.

"You did not quite finish," she said, dipping her fingers between his lips. He drew them into his mouth, whisking his tongue around them, and an eruption of desire throbbed low in her core.

They continued their meal, laughing and sharing stories as they proffered bites to one another, choosing from among the enormous variety of dishes Miles' cooks had prepared.

"Tell me about music," he asked at one point, leaning back in his chair to chew the dark bread she'd just fed him.

"Music?" She raised a slim eyebrow in question. "What of it?"

"I want to know why it stirs you as it does. How you learned to love it."

Catherine hesitated. She felt compelled to answer although doing so would reveal certain aspects of herself she normally preferred to keep separate from her lovers.

"My apologies," Miles said. "I meant not to probe."

"You haven't. 'Tis only I..." Conflict cast shadows of doubt through her mind. This was new territory for her, this sharing of information. Past lovers hadn't asked anything personal about her, nor she of them. It was an unspoken agreement that the exchange was physical, not emotional. To her surprise, she wanted to let Miles in, wanted him to know a bit about her.

"Forgive my impropriety," Miles repeated.

Catherine shook her head. "I'm flattered you asked. I simply wasn't expecting it."

"Nor was I," he admitted. "I don't...I normally don't care."

"But this time you do?"

He leaned forward once more, looking deep into her eyes. "Yes," he said quietly. "This time I do."

She selected a shard of cheese from the platter and held it before his lips. "Music is to me rather like this food. It satisfies a fundamental need. It stirs my passions and appeals to my most basic senses. When I hear beautiful music it quickens my heart and makes my blood race."

"Fascinating." He reached out to stroke a finger along her arm, raising goosebumps where he touched. "And when did you first discover you had such a reaction to music?"

"A friend..." His light caress made her squirm in her seat, clouding coherent thought. "A dear friend of mine introduced me. She said—ahhh."

"Yes?" He traced a path up to her throat, across her lips, and then down toward her breasts. A faint grin, full of mischief, touched the corners of his mouth, evidence that he enjoyed seductively torturing her. "What did she say?"

"She taught me to embrace my desires. She said if the music stirs me then I need to accept it, just as I need to accept everything in life that stirs me."

"Did she indeed?" He selected the last piece of beef from the platter and offered it to Catherine. As she took it, a drop of sauce fell on the corner of her bottom lip. Before she could press her napkin to it, Miles leaned forward, sweeping it up with the tip of his tongue. He did not draw away once he was finished, lingering instead by dotting small kisses across her lips as she chewed.

"And what of this?" he whispered, his breath flowing gently across her cheeks. "Does this stir you?"

"It does," she breathed. "Very much."

"So you accept it?"

"Completely."

He placed his hands on either side of her neck caressing her skin with his thumbs in slow, sensual circles before sliding upward to tease her earlobes, skating across the whorl of her outer ear. Once she'd swallowed the last bite, he brought her forward and seized her mouth with his.

Miles' lips were hot like embers, igniting Catherine's passion. She'd been simmering with desire all evening, her senses highly aroused by the intimate game they played. Now that they'd finished eating she unleashed her restraint, falling into his embrace and the heat of his desire.

His hands roamed everywhere, stroking, caressing, as though desperate to touch her all at once. She groaned in his mouth as he teased her nipples through her layers of clothing, rolling them between his fingers. She arched against him and pressed her breasts into his palms, craving the feel of him. She also wanted to touch him, to stroke her hands across his bronzed, warm skin.

Suddenly Miles broke the kiss. "Upstairs," he breathed, "Now."

"Yes."

They rose from their chairs without another word. Miles indicated the direction, and Catherine exited the dining room and walked up a flight of stairs on trembling legs as he trailed behind her. Her pulse spiked, agitated beats throbbing in her aching pussy. The start of a new relationship always filled her with an excited rush, although never before with such surprising force. It took every ounce of self-restraint she possessed not to turn around and demand Miles take her right there on the stairway.

They continued down the hall toward his bed chamber, the last door on the left.

For the briefest moment Catherine thought Miles hesitated, as though uncertain he really wanted her there. But then he opened the door and invited her inside, kissing her as he did so. Any doubt he may have had vanished as though it had never been.

He closed the door behind him with his foot, not releasing her mouth from his, pulling at her clothing as she tugged at his. They side-stepped across the room that way, mouths locked together. Miles grabbed fistfuls of her skirts in an effort to lift them, but the impatient attempt only resulted in the fabric swirling around her legs and becoming stubbornly entangled. As they reached the bed, Catherine broke away, able to savor a remnant of self-control so she could undress herself.

"Sit down." She nodded toward the bed.

Miles obeyed.

Catherine took a step backward, placing distance between them. "Patience, my lord," she said in response to his outstretched hand as he attempted to pull her back.

"I do not wish to be patient."

"Not even for this?" She lifted her skirts and removed one of her stockings, rolling it down her leg with agonizing slowness. She did the same with the other stocking and was rewarded with Miles' groan.

Next she removed the lace scarf tied about her throat and tossed it to him. It exposed the deep décolleté of her bodice, with her breasts seeming close to spilling out of the gown. She allowed Miles to enjoy it for only a moment before turning her back to him.

"I shall require your help," she said, thrilled seconds later by the sensual feel of his fingers unfastening tiny buttons on her outer gown.

He sprinkled kisses down the back of her neck as he worked. Once her dress was removed, he assisted her with the stays, petticoats, and chemise as well. When the last fabric dropped to the ground, he drew her naked body against him, her back to his chest. The small metal buttons on his shirt were blissfully cool against her heated skin.

"You leave me breathless," he whispered, pressing her buttocks against the rock-hard bulge straining beneath his breeches.

Catherine allowed her head to sink back against his shoulder, reveling in the contrast between her nude body and his fully clothed one. His hands cupped her breasts, stroking the silken skin. He teased her nipples, hardening them to granite peaks, pinching them lightly between his fingers.

A surge of desire stormed through her body, and her knees trembled like a newborn colt's. Desperate to touch him, she reached her arms up to encircle Miles' neck. He brought his head down as she did so, nibbling on her ear and shoulder before claiming her lips.

His kisses were hot, demanding. He pressed his mouth against hers with delicious force, parting her lips and slipping his tongue between them. Heat unfurled in her core and she groaned, longing for the feel of his skin sliding sensuously against hers. As if sensing her need, Miles broke the kiss and took her hand, leading her back to the bed.

She sat on the side of it, unashamedly naked as his heated gaze swept over her. His ragged exhalations mingled with the crackling wood in the fireplace. He nodded, almost as if he'd come to a decision. In a low voice he whispered, "You're as tempting as a siren to sailors. I cannot resist you."

Why would you want to? Confusion flitted through her mind. It was as if a glimmer of the hesitation she'd seen in him before made yet another appearance. Were secrets from Miles' past haunting him? He seemed to be grappling with a strong sense of guilt.

Yet they were both here, where they wanted to be, and she could see his hunger for her reflected in his eyes. She cast her bemusement aside. "Then do not. Instead, come join me."

He reached his hands toward her, guiding her down to lie supine upon the bed. With a gentle touch he cradled the back of her head to rest it lightly on the pillow. His fingers sifted through her hair, the long strands falling like wisps of black silk. Then, letting out a deep breath, he joined her.

Catherine sank into the mattress as Miles settled on top of her, the luxurious feeling of his weight making her heady with desire. Their kisses reached a new sense of urgency as passion took wing. Engulfed by the need to feel Miles' skin against hers, Catherine pulled at his shirt and waistcoat, wanting him as naked as she.

They broke apart for mere seconds as he hastily rid

himself of the offending garments. When the last of the clothing was discarded he lay back down on her, flooding her with ecstasy.

His skin was like heated silk overlaying marble. His muscles rippled and bunched as Catherine glided her hands over sensual power. His arms, his back, his shoulders, all perfectly sculpted into the man who was about to become her lover. She sighed with longing, aching for him to be inside of her.

Normally it was she who teased, who prolonged the mating, drawing out her lover's anticipation until he was ready to erupt. But this time the tables were turned. She was the eager one, desperate to join with him.

"I need you inside me," she breathed, parting her thighs. But to her surprise he shook his head, and she whimpered in frustration.

"Not yet, my love," he breathed, trailing his tongue along her breasts. "I have business to attend first."

"Business?"

"Oh, yes."

"Such as?" She inhaled a sharp hiss as he drew a nipple into his mouth and lightly pressed his teeth against the puckered flesh. Her heart slammed within her chest as if it were about to break free.

"Such as sucking the sweetness of your breasts." He shifted his attention from one to the other, pausing to lick the indentation at the base of her throat before taking the second nipple into his mouth.

"Mmm." He looked up at her. "Your skin is exquisite. Smooth as glass and so very soft."

He returned attention to her breast, licking around the nipple but this time holding off from sucking it into his mouth as she wanted. Instead, he tormented her by blowing on her fevered skin. She cried out and arched her back.

"Take it," she pleaded, her voice rising with desperation. She cared not a whit. Her nipples tightened and throbbed; she was desperate for him to relieve the feverish ache. Catherine burned, beads of sweat trickling between her breasts.

At last Miles showed mercy, drawing her distended nipple between his lips. He swirled his tongue around the pebbled bud, grazing it with his teeth. Her pussy clenched in response and moisture damped her thighs.

"Ah!" Engulfed with pleasure, Catherine groaned aloud as her hips began to sway and thrust against his pelvis. She slid her hands along the muscled slope of his back and down to his sides. Her fingers danced lightly across the ladder of his ribs, his skin soft as a newborn babe's. Then her hands traveled upward once more, along his forearms and biceps to his solid rock of shoulders.

"Now!" She wove her fingers through his hair and with a hand on either side of his head, lifted his gaze to hers. "I need you inside of me."

"Greedy woman," Miles teased, but he rose up, sitting back on his heels.

He grabbed one of myriad pillows tossed about his bed and propped it beneath Catherine's hips, raising her to him like an offering. He bent forward, positioning himself between her parted thighs. A wet path burned her skin where his lips and tongue kissed one knee and the inside of her leg. Tingles of desire raced down her spine, anticipation building as the warmth of his breath heated her thighs. Sweet, agonizing torture.

Miles edged his way toward her pussy, close but

not yet there. Warning bells of alarm clanged through her mind. What if he held off, ruthlessly teasing but failing to pleasure her aching clit? Panic surfaced. She squeezed her eyes shut, pinpricks of light dotting her vision. If only he were closer! Arched back, thrusting hips, willing him to end her torment. He was there, almost there, so close…

Sounds of her own shallow panting filled the room. Her clit throbbed; she was on fire for him. Heat from his breath washed over her pussy. She parted her thighs, wide as she could.

"Oh please, oh please…"

At last—*there!* Sweet, blessed relief as his tongue swept through the moist folds of her pussy and then, finally, swirled about her clit. He teased her softly at first, using just the tip of his tongue to flick at the engorged bud.

But he was as attuned to her needs as if he'd been her lover for years. He increased pressure exactly as she needed, reading her signals, his mind seemingly linked with hers. With his lips he kissed her pussy while continuing to swirl his tongue around her clit, faster and harder, drawing her ever closer toward release.

"Miles!"

She placed a hand on the back of his head, assurance that he'd stay, that this blissful torment would continue forever. With her other clenched hand she grabbed fistfuls of bed sheet, writhing on the mattress as she called out her lover's name. She was so close but she needed just a little more…

She thrust her hips forward and just as she did so, Miles sank two fingers deep in her pussy.

Ecstasy devoured her, wrapping every inch of her

body in divine sensation. Her ragged moans filled the room, growing louder every second as Miles drove into her. He lifted his head and pierced her with his stare as he repeatedly plunged his fingers in and out, the palm of his hand pounding her clit as his fingers pleasured her slick vaginal walls.

"I can't get enough of watching you," he murmured. "You're so beautiful. So sensual."

"It's you, my lord," Catherine panted. "You who make me beautiful."

"I want to watch you come." He added a third finger. "Now."

"No!" She gasped from the onslaught of sensation, spiraling toward release, but with sheer force of will held back.

"I need you inside of me. Fill me, Miles. Please. Then I shall come."

A wicked smile crept across his lips. "And so you shall."

He withdrew his fingers and crept forward, gently aligning himself on top of her, resting much of his weight on his arms. Catherine looked up at his face, beads of sweat dotting his brow, and her moisture yet lingering on his lips. Hunger reflected in his eyes, and for a brief moment, satisfaction rang sweet that his hunger was entirely for her.

He reached between them, nudging the thick tip of his cock against her entrance, gathering juices, and then at last, in one, swift movement, buried himself in her fire.

She was so deliciously filled by him, her pussy stretched wide, almost to the point of pain, yet not. His cock pounded her with smooth, hard strokes, engulfing her with his power, bringing her senses alive. She inhaled his musky fragrance, tasted the salt on his lips from where he'd sucked her clit.

Her splayed hands once more skated down the curve of Miles' back to the slope of his ass, thrilled by the erotic clench and release of his muscles as he repeatedly plunged into her eager pussy. His passion-stained eyes looked deeply into hers. She met his gaze as well until her eyes refused to stay open against the first flutters of her approaching release.

"Come for me, Catherine." His breaths were ragged and she knew he was close as well.

He increased the speed of their mating, burying himself to his balls and then drawing back out, again and again. The rush of her shallow pants echoed in her ears as she climbed higher, teetering on the verge of release. He drove against her pussy and she tightened her thighs around his waist, needing him inside her even deeper, craving the blissful stretch of his cock against her slick walls.

Her heartbeat thundered against her ribcage until at last she could hold off no more, crying out as the orgasm consumed her, throbbing pulses crashing over her like waves. With one final thrust, Miles joined her over the edge.

For several moments afterward, he stayed atop her, infusing her with his heady scent. His labored breathing whooshed against her ear, gradually slowing as seconds ticked by. At last she summoned the will to shift her hips from beneath his, and he responded with a quarter turn roll to relieve her of his weight.

He remained alongside her, casually stroking her leg with his foot, but the warmth from his heated body gradually faded, like the remnants of glowing embers.

Catherine looked over at Miles with a smile tugging her lips. "I suppose that shall have to suffice as dessert."

"I beg your pardon?"

She stretched like a cat and rolled to her side. Propping herself on one arm, she looked down at Miles. "I won't deny the dinner was divine. And after dinner...well, it was nearly like heaven." She touched her lips to his, almost as if to thank him. "But there is one thing you must know about me if this relationship is to continue."

"Oh?" He propped himself up as well, a quizzical expression lining his face. And what is that?"

"I adore sweets."

"Do you?"

"Most decidedly. And it seems a terrible shame after the divine meal we shared that the sweets have been ignored."

He maintained an expression of stoic solemnity. "Indeed, 'twould be a shame. But perhaps it is not too late to right the situation."

He rose from the bed to tug at a bell hanging just above his head. Within minutes there came a discreet knock upon the door. Miles donned a silk wrap and answered. Brief words were exchanged Catherine could not hear, but seconds later Miles returned to the bed bearing a silver platter topped with a vast assortment of almond pastes and mini fruit tarts.

His somber countenance yet firmly in place, he held the platter before her. "Your dessert, Miss Sheffield."

Catherine was so surprised she laughed aloud.

"You knew!" she exclaimed, reaching for a tart.

Miles set the tray on the bed between them and took one of the sweets for himself. "At the ball you ate naught but dessert."

"How ill-mannered of me." She bit into the flaky crust, groaning aloud as bits of sweet apple filled her mouth. "Although I make no apologies for my enjoyment."

"I admire a lady who takes what she wants."

Catherine plucked a second tart from the tray. "I am surprised you noticed what I ate."

Miles' eyes darkened at once as he leaned closer to Catherine and brushed his lips across hers. "I noticed everything about you that evening."

She returned the kiss, deepening it, enjoying the taste of sugared fruit upon his tongue. Suddenly a cool, sticky substance rubbed across her breast. She looked down. Miles had taken one of the fruit tarts and pressed the top of it against her skin, smearing her with the thick preserves.

Her breath caught in her throat. "What a mess you've made."

"My deepest apologies." He placed a hand upon her shoulder and leaned her back against the pillows. "You must allow me to clean it at once."

He took her breast in his mouth, swirling his tongue against the fruit-coated nipple, sucking her until every bit was gone. Her pulse quickened.

"What a fine way to have dessert," Miles breathed, picking up another fruit tart. He dipped his fingers into it and smeared her other breast.

Catherine's eyes fluttered closed, at once ready to receive him, but before they made love again she suddenly needed to know, with certainty, that she would see him again.

"Have dinner with me next week," she gasped, barely able to maintain control of her senses as Miles' tongue swirled around her nipple.

"Anytime." He smeared more fruit on her skin, this time on her stomach.

"No," she groaned, arching her hips as his fingers grazed her clit. "I mean, come to a dinner party. Next week."

Miles stilled, and Catherine realized her invitation had taken their relationship in another direction, beyond a discreet affair. It startled her that she'd made the request, but at the same time it was what she desired. Never mind she'd not done so with other lovers. She wanted Audrey to meet Miles and would not dwell on the reasons behind it.

He nodded his acceptance, and she exhaled a breath of relief. She guessed he was as surprised to receive her invitation as she was to extend it, but nonetheless he also appeared to welcome it, and for that she was oddly grateful.

Miles cast her a wicked grin as he resumed his fruit tart painting across her skin. Embers of desire stirred to life once more. She glanced down, his rock hard cock pressed against her thigh, and she smiled like a contented cat. Miles Hawkins seemed to want her as much as she wanted him.

****

The din of men's voices swirled about the room like the heady smoke from their clay pipes. Behind the counter, an attendant brewed coffee, the thick, pungent drink now as common as ale. From his position at one of several long benches lining the length of the room, Miles enjoyed the company of friends and strangers alike. It was their usual afternoon gathering at Tom's, just one among thousands of coffee shops in town.

He took a sip of his drink and pointed his pipe at James Norris. "You mark my words, Norris." He stabbed the air for emphasis. "The Americans will have their independence from us before long. 'Tis inevitable."

"But we've already defeated them at Charleston and Camden."

"That does not make it right."

"Not saying it does," Norris agreed, puffing his pipe. "But we view the outcome differently. Our boys are fighting well."

"The Americans defeated us at Vincennes last year," Miles reminded his friend.

Norris was about to respond when a man approaching their table interrupted the conversation.

"Clifton." Norris nodded a greeting to the newcomer. "Good to see you."

"And you," the man replied.

"Please. Sit." Norris moved over to accommodate him and turned toward Miles. "Do you know the Earl of Clifton?"

"Haven't had the pleasure."

Norris made swift introductions and the men nodded greetings to one another. Clifton set down his cup and leaned his arms atop the table.

"Lively debate you've got going," he commented, referring to their conversation about the Revolution. "Have to say I agree with you, Norris. I don't see the Americans defeating our British might anytime soon."

Norris laughed. "Nor do I, but Hawkins has an uncanny ability to predict the outcome of political matters."

Clifton sipped his coffee and nodded toward Miles. "Odd I haven't seen you around before. Do you come to Tom's often?"

"I do. Past several months anyway."

"How remarkable that we've not crossed paths." Clifton turned to blow pipe smoke in the air then faced Miles once more. "Tell me, Hawkins, why have you—"

"I've been away." His swift interruption made it clear that further questions would not be welcome.

As conversation came to a temporary halt, Norris intervened.

"You and Hawkins have a common acquaintance," he said to the earl.

"Indeed? And who might that be?"

"Miss Catherine Sheffield. I believe you know her, do you not, Clifton?"

At the mention of Catherine's name the earl's face took on a pleasant grin. "Ah, the incomparable Miss Sheffield. Why, yes, I've had the good fortune of knowing her."

Perhaps it was his imagination, but Miles was sure Clifton put a slight emphasis on the word "knowing," suggesting there was or had been more to his relationship with Catherine than a mere superficial acquaintance. A slow burn of rage began simmering in his blood.

Norris, unaware of the reaction he'd caused in his friend, continued blithely along. "I introduced Catherine to Hawkins at the Kenworth ball a fortnight ago."

Clifton sipped his coffee and licked his lips, almost as though recalling Catherine's taste. Red haze clouded Miles' vision. A muscle twitched in the back of his jaw.

"She and I used to spend a bit of time together, and I regret lately her schedule has allowed us no further engagements. But a more elegant and, dare I say, *worldly* woman I have yet to meet. Would you not agree, Hawkins?"

Tension filled the room like dense fog. Norris shot a look at Miles, his narrowed eyes making it clear he recognized the effect Clifton's words were having on his friend. He swung his attention back over to Clifton. "I understand your diary is rather full up as well," Norris said.

Clifton raised a casual eyebrow. "Indeed?"

"In the company of Miss Felicity Penworth."

"Ah, yes," Clifton confirmed, shrugging. "Well, since Miss Sheffield has become unavailable, I do what I must." He sat back in his seat and drew a long puff from his pipe. Blowing a plume of smoke in the air, he continued, "I'm quite enjoying Miss Penworth's company, as have others. She's certainly acquainted with a great deal of people and can spin quite a tale when so inclined." He chuckled aloud, as if recalling an amusing story.

Turning to Miles, he asked, "Have you had the pleasure of Miss Penworth's company as well, Hawkins?"

With anger sizzling his blood, Miles rose from the bench and spoke directly to Norris. "I shall see you tomorrow."

"Off so soon?"

Miles ignored Clifton as he strode smoothly across

the room and out the door. As soon as the fresh air hit him it began clearing his head and easing some of the urge he'd felt to pound the earl senseless. The pompous ass deserved no less.

Although as Miles strolled down the street toward home, he did wonder from where the unexpected jealousy arose. His relationship with Catherine, after all, was just what he wanted. No tiresome requirement to court her and assume the proper role of suitor. No uncomfortable meetings with her parents as his family and background were subject to undue scrutiny for determining whether he would suit as a husband. The boundaries of their relationship satisfied them both without the dreary obligation of promises and future.

He turned the corner and walked along the park, vaguely aware that his last thought brought him more unease than it did comfort. Why should that be?

Miles knew what he wanted, and it did not include commitment of any kind. He'd had it once before—the commitment, the promise—and it had nearly killed him. When he'd finally emerged from it, bloodied and battered but nonetheless whole, he knew the kind of man he would be and even made himself a pledge.

Never again would emotions for a woman sink their dangerous talons into his heart. Not that he'd refrain from enjoying the physical aspects of a woman's company, but that's as far as he would allow himself to go. Ever again.

As for his feelings toward Catherine...well, they weren't feelings, not exactly. It was just that he was not inclined to hear of her previous conquests. As long as she was with him he would be the only man she'd know. The Earl of Clifton could go to the devil. The fool had had her once but lost her, and from the way he'd acted, it had been Catherine's decision, not his.

Miles squared his shoulders and turned the corner toward home, satisfied he now understood his reaction to Clifton in the coffee house. When the time came for he and Catherine to part ways, they would each do whatever they pleased. But for now Catherine was his, and as long as they were together he gamely vowed there would be no other.

****

"Believe me, Catherine, you would have been horrified. My pet poodle could have played that concerto better, and yet Lord Watley is the toast of the town for his supposed virtuosic playing. Truly, it boggles the mind. I left in the middle of the concert it was so unbearable."

Catherine pasted on a smile. Ordinarily she would have enjoyed Lady Eleanor Tetley's sharp critique of a violin player of whom neither woman was particularly fond, but this evening was different.

She awaited Miles.

Struggling to focus her attention on the conversation at hand, Catherine risked a quick look over her shoulder toward the doorway to see whether she could spot his arrival. So far, nothing.

"Do not fret." Audrey's comment was whispered into Catherine's left ear.

Catherine turned and smiled at her friend, grateful Audrey knew her so well and understood how she was feeling. This evening would be the first time Audrey would meet one of Catherine's paramours, and Audrey's opinion of Miles mattered more than she cared to admit.

"Lord Miles Hawkins."

The announcement was made by Audrey's butler in the same flat tone he used to announce all the other guests, yet to Catherine's ear it was like the sound of a symphony. Her heart raced with anticipation.

With as much restraint as she could muster she walked to Miles' side, then thought she would melt as his scorching gaze held her like a prisoner.

He said nothing prior to brushing a searing kiss across the back of her hand, making her heart somersault as he did so.

"You look exquisite," he murmured at last.

The compliment pleased her, yet she was puzzled by an uneasy glimmer in Miles' eyes. There was no time to say anything for Audrey approached.

Catherine turned to her dearest friend. "Audrey, may I introduce Lord Miles Hawkins. Lord Miles, this is Lady Audrey Sheffield."

Miles bowed low. "A pleasure, my lady."

"And mine as well, Lord Miles," Audrey replied. "Catherine has spoken highly of you."

"Has she?" He stole a sideways glance at Catherine and an enigmatic smile touched his lips, though failed to reach his eyes. "Then I must do all I can to ensure I remain in her favor."

His response flattered, yet Catherine couldn't shake the sense that Miles' comment held more than what appeared on the surface. She had no time to respond, however, for more guests arrived and diverted Audrey's attention. As she stepped away to greet them, other newcomers approached Catherine, and she spent the next several minutes introducing Miles to Audrey's dinner party guests.

His grace and charm garnered him numerous invitations for future occasions, yet all the while Catherine felt certain something was amiss. Miles maintained the calm demeanor of a contented dinner guest, but it seemed as though his politesse masked trouble that simmered furiously, just barely out of sight.

Audrey's butler announced dinner, and the guests took their places. Miles was seated to Catherine's right and Lord Samuel Farley occupied the place to her left. Such an arrangement ordinarily would have pleased her for she'd always enjoyed Lord Farley's witty company, but this evening her preoccupation with Miles kept even the smallest pleasures at bay.

"Tell us Lord Miles," Audrey spoke from her seat at the front of the table, "how do you plan on spending your summer?"

"With friends, Lady Sheffield." His gaze captured Catherine's for a moment. "I find no matter what the occasion, 'tis always enhanced by the company one keeps."

"Hear, hear," Lord Farley echoed Miles' sentiment. "A truer statement could not be made."

The conversation continued on that theme, but Catherine scarcely heard it. The guarded look Miles had given her, albeit brief, carried unspoken meaning. Something had happened, she was sure of it. There was a difference in him not there before. He was edgy, and tense.

Catherine could not put a finger on it, but Miles almost acted as though he had been...*threatened*? But by what? And by whom? Whatever it was, she longed for a moment alone so she could find out what vexed him.

At long last, after dinner and port and conversation and music, the evening drew to a close, and the guests prepared to leave. Catherine had, as always, her own carriage on hand, but as she awaited the maid to bring her shawl, Miles spoke low in her ear. "I would request the honor of escorting you home."

The request was unusual; he knew she drove herself. Still, his words carried in them an undercurrent of need.

She nodded her agreement. "Very well. I shall send my driver on."

She gave Audrey a brief kiss and thanked her for the dinner.

"Lovely as ever," Catherine told her friend.

"I am so glad you could come, my dear." She turned toward Miles. "It was a pleasure to meet you, Lord Miles. I hope to see you again soon."

"As do I, my lady." Miles brushed a chaste kiss across the back of Audrey's hand before he and Catherine stepped outside.

Catherine's thoughts swirled. She was grateful Audrey withheld comment on her agreement to be escorted home but knew her friend would certainly be wondering why. Had she, too, sensed something peculiar in Miles? Or was it simply that Audrey knew Catherine well and could sense the sizzling air of passion between her and the enigmatic Miles Hawkins? That alone would be all the explanation Audrey required.

Tranquility permeated the evening air. Since Catherine and Miles were the last guests to leave, the usual crush of other carriages was absent, leaving behind only the occasional call of night birds. Without a word spoken between them they alighted in Miles' carriage. He tapped on the window and the horses lurched forward.

Catherine waited another minute before speaking, sensing she would be the one to address whatever tension was between them even though Miles was the one who'd created it. "Miles—"

His bruising kiss nearly knocked the wind out of her. She gasped, and it seemed Miles responded with what could only be described as a growl. Before Catherine could even think he was on top of her, pressing her down upon the seat, anchoring her in place with the weight of his body. His hands were everywhere, caressing her face, her breasts, sliding down to skim her thighs. He kissed with feral passion, plunging his tongue into her mouth, then nipping the downy skin of her neck.

His ferocity made her head swim, and she was excited as never before. Her heart slammed within her chest like a drum. Blood roared in her ears and her pussy gushed with sizzling pulses of arousal. Still, through the erotic haze clouding coherent thought, Catherine wanted to know what had brought on Miles' behavior.

"What," she hissed as his probing fingers found her nipple, "has happened?"

"Mine," he growled. He continued to kiss and caress, passionate yet agonizingly sensual while the carriage pitched and swayed.

His rock hard cock pressed into her abdomen. He shifted his weight to allow space between their bodies and reached down to shove aside the restrictive clothing. His erection sprang free and he slid down so he could grasp her skirts and lift them, exposing her calves, her thighs, and finally, her burning core.

As his gaze swept over her he groaned low in his throat, like a note of approval. Then he bent forward and buried his face between her thighs, his tongue sweeping through her sleek folds and across her clitoris, making her cry aloud.

When he shifted upward once more, he licked his way down her throat and along the delicate collarbone. With one hand he pulled her dress down off her shoulders, exposing her breasts. He swirled his tongue around the dusky pink areola before sucking a distended nipple between his lips.

As he pleasured her he reached out a hand to grasp one of hers, guiding it between their bodies to his jutting shaft.

"Touch me," he rasped. "Please."

Desperation she didn't understand coated his voice. Nevertheless, she did as Miles asked, grasping hold of his cock and stroking. His reaction was immediate as his eyelids drifted shut, and he sucked in air. She loved the way he felt in her hand, so hard, so hot. His sex pulsed in response to her touch and his hips swayed as she stroked.

"Faster," he growled, emitting a low, guttural groan. He acted as though fire fueled his veins, although she had no idea what had triggered his sudden, dangerous lust.

Any further thought flew like the wind from her mind when his fingers slipped between her thighs and found their way to the wet folds of her slit. With quick light strokes he rubbed her clit and plunged two fingers deep into her pussy.

Elizabeth Shore

Her body trembled and she gasped, grinding her hips against his hand as much as the small space allowed. Release was seconds away. Miles thrust his stiff cock harder in her grip, and from his ragged breathing, he was close as well. But suddenly she sensed the carriage slowing and realized they must be nearly there.

"Miles, stop," she whispered, quiet yet forceful so he would understand.

He lifted his head and looked around. As he blew out a ragged breath he became instantly calm, almost eerily so considering what had just occurred. He eased away from Catherine and helped her into a sitting position, straightening her skirts before hiking up his breeches. Seconds later, the carriage came to a stop, and Miles' driver leapt down to the graveled ground.

The door swung open, and the driver extended a hand into the carriage to assist Catherine out. Miles followed quickly behind and instructed the driver to take the horse and carriage into the stable—his stable.

Catherine turned to Miles, her emotions suddenly cool. "I thought you were escorting me home."

"I will. Later." He whisked her hand into his and turned toward the door.

She dug in her heels. "No one drags me where I do not wish to go."

"You do not care for my home?"

She withdrew her hand from his. "'Tis not that. I am merely trying to understand what has come over you this evening."

The dangerous tenseness returned. She could see it in his eyes by the way they darkened to the color of pitch, and she could see it in his body as if every muscle had turned to stone.

For several moments Miles said nothing, like he was weighing in his mind what to tell her and what to keep secret. A muscle twitched in the back of his jaw and the expression on his faced clouded, as if an unpleasant memory had newly surfaced.

"I met your friend this afternoon. The Earl of Clifton."

"George?" Catherine's surprise upon hearing mention of the earl forced a momentary loss of proper etiquette as she casually used his first name.

Miles' eyes narrowed. "Let me amend what I said. I met your *very good friend* the Earl of Clifton."

Catherine recovered her composure nearly as quickly as it had left her. "And what of it?" she asked evenly. "Am I not entitled to have friends?"

Miles stepped forward and grasped Catherine around the waist, pulling her against him. "Not *those* kinds of friends," he seethed, capturing her lips in a hard kiss.

If she wasn't so incensed by his unwarranted possession she would have become lost in bone-melting lust. No one, ever, had kissed her like Miles.

Catherine twisted out of his grasp. "How dare you!" she snapped. "Whatever I have done in the past and whomever I choose to associate with is none of your concern."

"Oh, but you are wrong, Miss Sheffield," Miles replied, his voice dangerously soft. "Everything you do is of my concern, and as long as you are with me, you are *mine*."

His eyes glittered in the darkness, his expression fierce. He stepped forward and pulled Catherine into his embrace, this time with a tenderness that had been absent moments before. Although she knew she ought to resist, fighting him was as useless as trying to ward off sleep when in the grip of exhaustion. Catherine sank into his embrace, allowing Miles to kiss her breathless.

At last he paused, lifting his mouth from hers but easing away only enough to put a finger's space between them. His arms remained around her waist, holding her close as though afraid she would run. Fortunately, she sensed the red fog of anger he'd carried moments before was loosening its grip.

"You are right," he conceded, breathing into her hair. "Your friends are your own. But for however long you and I choose to remain together, you will belong to me. I will share you with no other."

For a brief moment, Catherine tensed. This was not supposed to be. She wanted no entanglements with any of her lovers. Whenever she sensed one of them start to become possessive she broke off the relationship like snapping a twig from a tree. So what was it about Miles' demands that sent tingles of desire coursing through her veins?

She looked up at him, nodding. "Agreed. But the same applies to you. I will not have you cavorting about town with other lovers when you are involved with me. Once our relationship is over..." She let the sentence remain unfinished, uninterested in considering that eventuality.

He pressed his lips tight as if he, too, did not care to discuss that aspect any further. Instead he lifted a finger and traced a line down the length of her throat, swirling sensual patterns over her skin. "Come to bed with me."

"I'd love to."

This time, Catherine brooked no resistance as she allowed Miles to escort her inside his stately home. As expected, Evans awaited them inside, but Miles waved the man away.

Unable to pause long enough to discard their wraps, he immediately led Catherine upstairs and into his bedroom. Their shadows danced on the wall in the flames of numerous candles lit by Miles' ever-attentive staff. After shutting the door behind them, he set to disrobing her with fingers so impatient they shook.

She was just as eager, craving his skin against hers, the smooth, manly heat enveloping her like fire. She tugged at his waistcoat, pulling it sharply down and away from his arms once the last button was released. Tossing it onto the floor, she immediately went to work on his shirt, pulling it up and over his head.

At last, the silken skin she hungered for was hers to savor. Pressing her lips against his muscled chest, she licked a track from one nipple to the next, rewarded with his throaty groan. She loved his heated skin scorching her lips and how the saltiness of his sweat tingled her tongue, as if she were tasting his very essence.

As she kissed him, her fingers undid the fastenings on his breeches. Once free, she lifted her lips from his chest and locked her gaze with his. With unhurried deliberation, she slid down his breeches, kissing her way along every inch of skin she exposed.

When his cock sprang free, she slid her tongue along its entire length, loving the connection with this most intimate part of him. With excruciating slowness she wrapped her lips around his rock hard shaft, bit by bit drawing it deeper into her mouth. His low, helpless groan rewarded her.

As she pleasured him by sliding her lips down and back along the entire length of his cock, she delicately fondled his balls, using the tips of her fingers to tease and caress them. His male, musky scent surrounded her as he stiffened even further under her attention.

Gently, he placed his hand against the back of her head, guiding her, rocking his pelvis in and out of her wet lips. His moans grew steadily in volume as they echoed about the bedchamber until, suddenly, he pulled himself back.

"No more," he panted, his voice ragged as he looked down at her, "or I shall spill my seed far too soon."

She rose, smiling, immeasurably pleased by the compliment.

Like an experienced courtesan she pressed her body sensuously against his as they tumbled into bed, knowing he could feel the lushness of her breasts against him. His throaty groans rewarded her as his fingers flew over the buttons of her dress to undo them. At last the prohibitive clothing was removed, and she reveled in the voluptuous, searing contact of skin as their bodies joined together as though fused.

Catherine felt as if she were spiraling out of control. Miles' powerful embrace enveloped her like a sensual cloak as he kissed her endlessly, his mouth and lips scorching her with fire. He inched down her body, kissing her breasts, laving her nipple with his tongue. She wound her thighs about his waist, pressing herself wantonly against him. She could wait no longer.

"I must have you, Miles. Now." She cried out as he

trailed his tongue along the downy sides of her breast.

He acquiesced, leaning forward to place his elbows on either side of her head. He rested his weight on his arms and held her face between his hands. Positioning his cock at the entrance to her pussy, he plunged inside.

Catherine heard his tortured groan as she sheathed him in her core, the walls of her pussy slick with need. He withdrew nearly all the way before thrusting hard again. His arms trembled on either side of her. She suspected he was trying to hold back as much as possible, though she herself teetered on the edge of release.

Miles pounded inside of her, every movement building desire. He made love to her with an intense fierceness, as if to make a point, branding her as his through the frenzy of their mating. He was fierce, relentless.

Catherine responded in kind, arching her hips to meet his thrusts, wrapping her arms around him to keep him close. Sizzles of desire roared through her body as she hovered on the edge of release. It was there, almost there. The sound of Miles' guttural groans filled her ears as he drove into her, his balls slapping her feverish skin. Her eyelids fluttered closed and she sank her fingernails into his sweat-slickened back, driving him deeper into her needy pussy.

Seconds later, passion erupted. Catherine cried aloud over and over, seized by the hot pulses of orgasm. Miles immediately followed, shuddering atop her as he spilled his seed.

Afterward, Catherine sank in the crook of Miles' arm as he held her tightly against him, their legs coiled together like vines. With one of his fingers, Miles slowly caressed her cheek, but after a time he went still and his slow, steady breathing floated through the room like a whisper.

Her heart and mind filled with drowsy contentment. She smiled in the dark room. It seemed as if she and Miles had reached an understanding, something they both easily agreed upon and which afforded them a surprising sense of comfort. For however long their relationship lasted, the two of them would belong only to each other.

Chapter Five

"Lord Miles is here, miss."

"Send him in, Hannah." Catherine swallowed her last bite of scone and brushed crumbs from her lips as her heartbeat quickened. Smoothing her skirts, she rose from the table just as Miles walked through the door.

In only a few long strides he stood before her, sweeping her into his embrace. His lips were warm and eager, as though it had been days since he last kissed her rather than mere hours. A flush of arousal slid through her veins, and she broke away to smile up at him. "You're early."

"I couldn't wait." He kissed her again, seeming not to care whether the servants or anyone else should happen to see them.

Catherine sighed. It had been this way for weeks now, this urgent, consuming need they had for one another. She had expected the excitement of newly found passion and the initial thrill with Miles to eventually cool and then subside as it had with all others. Yet just the opposite seemed to have occurred.

Her happiest moments of the day were the hours spent with him, and the loneliest occurred whenever they were apart. Not only was he an extraordinary lover, that was without dispute. But the connection she felt with him, as if a piece of her soul had gone missing and then reunited with Miles, was a feeling she'd never before known.

Weeks ago, ever since the fiery discussion and subsequent lovemaking in which they declared fealty to one another for the extent of their relationship, it had periodically occurred to Catherine that she was ignoring her own rules of the game. She saw Miles nearly every day, and she invited him to her home. They were seen together at social occasions. She even abandoned her personal requirement that she always bring her own carriage and driver wherever she went in favor of allowing Miles to act as escort.

In the back her mind, warning signs were alive and well. Whispers of John's name, like a ghostly haunting, reminded her of a time long ago when a man's possession had ensnared her like a trap.

Never again, she had vowed. Never again. So what was she doing with Miles? She tried to convince herself it was only temporary, that the long hours she spent with him cast no more meaning on their relationship than the one she'd enjoyed with, say, the Earl of Clifton.

But for all the effort Catherine put into that assertion, the real truth refused to go away. She was falling in love with Miles Hawkins and was helpless to stop it.

She would say nothing to him, of course. Feelings between them were not supposed to occur. Besides, stubborn as she was, Catherine clung to the faint yet illogical hope that if she refused to acknowledge her feelings out loud it would somehow prevent them from truly existing.

The click of Hannah's approaching footsteps returned her thoughts to the present. With a gentle yet firm hand she broke free of Miles' embrace just as her maid entered the breakfast room.

"A note for you, miss," Hannah said, proffering the folded parchment atop a silver tray.

Catherine took the message, the insignia stamp in the wax seal indicating it was from Audrey.

Dismissing Hannah, Catherine sat back down at the dining table and invited Miles to do the same. Her cheeks burned from their ardent embrace and a surge of happiness made her feel light as air. They'd made plans to attend another concert in the park that afternoon, and the combination of Mozart's music and Miles' company pleased Catherine like nothing else in the world.

As she read the scant words in Audrey's note, her sunny day suddenly clouded. A dark sense of foreboding drained her exuberance.

Dearest Catherine,

I must speak with you at once. Something has happened of which you need to be aware. Make haste.

Yours, Audrey

Despite the summer warmth, Catherine shivered. Audrey's summons could mean only one thing— Simon. He must have done something, or was about to do something, that would affect her. She could not imagine what it was, but certainly nothing good.

Miles set down the cup of tea he'd been drinking and grasped Catherine by the shoulders, likely noticing her sudden change.

"What is it? Tell me."

Catherine shook her head. How could she? Miles knew nothing of her former life, of the fact that she used to be Lucy Underhill. Or used to be married. That she was not Audrey's niece, and her deceased husband's brother wanted to hunt her down like a dog taking a stag.

Those were secrets only she and Audrey knew, and she meant to keep it that way. *Had* to keep it that way. Simon could never discover her whereabouts.

"I—'Tis nothing, really. But please forgive me, Miles. I must cancel today's plans. I need to see Audrey."

"'Tis no bother. I shall take you." He rose from his chair, preparing to leave. But it could not be.

"No. I will go alone."

In an instant, his eyes lost their sparkle, shadowed instead by a cloud of hurt. He reared back, almost seeming to flinch from her words, and his abrupt transformation showed Catherine only too well how she'd wounded him. She may as well have pierced her own heart. After weeks of their being inseparable, she'd shut him out with seemingly no more thought than closing a door. He had to find the change in her behavior unexpected. How could it not affect him?

Miles waited for a moment, perhaps wondering if she would offer an explanation. Then his expression altered once more and the hurt was erased as coolly and calmly as if he'd donned a mask. In its place slid cold detachment, worn like protective armor.

"Very well," he said with a quick, parting nod. He turned to pick up his hat from atop a chair and made his leave.

But suddenly, Catherine could not bear the thought of dealing with Audrey's disturbing news while reeling from the ache in her heart. She raced toward the doorway. "Miles, wait."

He paused but did not turn around. Beneath his elegantly tailored frock coat the corded muscles in his shoulders tensely bunched.

She stood in front of him and placed her palms against his chest to be certain he would not leave.

"There are things about me—"

"That I do not need to know."

"But..." She could not think what to say. He was making it too easy.

"We each have our secrets, Catherine. Likely they are painful or difficult to speak of... 'Tis why they are secrets."

From the depths of his eyes shone the haunting pain that had revealed itself to her several times before, though she still did not know the cause behind it.

"You have your own," she whispered.

He nodded. "Months ago, at the concert in St. James', you spared me from speaking of something I wish to keep silent. 'Tis only right I do the same for you."

Unshed tears pooled in her eyes. What was the pain he insisted on hiding? Was it time for both of them to share their secrets and begin together to heal? But that would mean taking their relationship in an entirely new direction—one neither of them wanted to explore. Wasn't that what they agreed?

"I will contact you as soon as I return."

He kissed her again, tenderly this time, a kiss that encompassed more than just physical passion. A kiss that held promises.

"Be safe, Catherine."

This time she let him go, watching him walk quietly out the door and away from her home. Though she was anxious about her upcoming conversation with Audrey, she also carried with her a bright spot of hope. When she returned, Miles would be waiting.

****

"'Tis about Simon, I know. Tell me what he's done," Catherine uttered the minute she walked through Audrey's door, but her friend would have none of it.

"Take off your wrap and sit down, Catherine. We shall at least begin in a civilized manner, despite the topic we discuss."

Audrey's calm composure steadied Catherine's nerves but just barely. She did as requested and deposited her wrap with Audrey's maid, then followed her friend into the sitting room where refreshments awaited.

The weather had turned dark and stormy, prohibiting them from enjoying Audrey's garden outdoors. It was probably just as well, Catherine mused, taking her seat. She would find no pleasure in anything at the moment.

Audrey poured tea for them both and served Catherine one of the delicate almond cakes she adored.

"You are correct," Audrey acknowledged only after they were settled and had emptied half their cups. "This is about Simon. He plans to marry."

For a moment Catherine was buoyed by a sense of hope, thinking Simon's pending nuptials meant he'd given up looking for her and turned his attention elsewhere.

"He plans on marrying Jane Denbigh."

Catherine gasped; her mouth fell open as optimism shattered like glass. Had Audrey stabbed a dagger in her heart she could not have been more surprised. The news was like a proclamation from hell. Jane Denbigh. Her dear childhood friend. She sat back in her chair stunned, as if she'd been kicked.

"No, not Jane," she whispered. "That cannot be."

The cup in her hand shook against the saucer, rattling like bones. She set it atop the table and stared at Audrey. Slowly her shock gave way to anger and then rage. Her blood boiled in her veins.

"She's just a child," she growled.

"She's sixteen, Catherine. The same age as you when you married. Since John's passing, Simon is now heir and he plans to have a wife. He's even taken up residence in your former home." Audrey sipped her tea, her expression hard.

An eerie similarity existed between what had happened to Catherine and was about to happen to Jane Denbigh. Jane's family was not one of money. A nobleman such as Simon Underhill, although merely of baronial rank, far exceeded what the Denbighs dared hope for as their eldest girl's groom.

Although Jane was young she was marriageable age, and what parent in their situation would refuse a marriage proposal from a nobleman? 'Twas likely they were overcome with joy, not knowing, of course, that Simon Underhill would eat their daughter alive.

"He must be stopped."

Audrey's face was dark as slowly she shook her head. "I have been trying to think of a way to prevent this marriage since I first learned of it. There are no grounds for objection."

Catherine shot up from her chair and paced about the sitting room, her fingers curled into fists. "He'll beat Jane. You know he will."

"As is his right." Audrey's cold words were like a death knell. Kind and quiet Jane being subject to Simon's wrath...there *must* be a way to stop it. Her mind spun, churning through every possible consideration.

"A woman can divorce her husband for cruelty," she said aloud as she returned to her seat.

"But she cannot stop a marriage on the grounds he *may* be cruel," Audrey countered. "It has to happen first."

Hope sputtered like a flame about to expire, yet Catherine would not allow its demise. A way to stop Simon existed. She simply had to find it.

Suddenly something sparked in the back of her mind, the tiniest flicker of memory. Her focus shifted, bearing down, trying to get it to surface. Something Audrey had told her not long ago. Something about John. And Simon...

There! She had it. She swung around in her chair to face Audrey. "You said recently Simon and John used to travel to London frequently but then stopped. Something about a scandal?"

"That's right." Audrey nodded and waited for Catherine to go on, confusion wrinkling her brow.

"If we could find out what the scandal was," Catherine mused aloud, "and use it to our advantage..."

Audrey gasped. "Gadzooks, you're not talking of blackmail, are you?"

"Of course not," Catherine reassured, but her voice held an edge. "Not exactly, anyway. I shouldn't propose something quite so sordid. But if we possessed information Simon wishes we did not, well..." She shrugged. "I just think perhaps he could be persuaded to change his mind about marrying Jane. 'Tis all I meant."

Concern was etched deeply in the contours of Audrey's face. "Even if you learned of the scandal, what then? You cannot reveal yourself to Simon, Catherine. It could mean your death. I shall contact him on your behalf."

"No."

"Catherine, I—"

"The answer is no." Catherine leaned forward and grasped Audrey's hands in a firm grip. "I am unwavering on that point. If you contact Simon he will without question seek you out in London, and he'll demand you tell him of my whereabouts."

"I never would."

"You would not want to, I know," Catherine replied softly. "But nothing is beyond Simon Underhill. He is cruel to the marrow. Your life would be in danger, Audrey." Her throat grew tight and she swallowed back a hard lump.

"You've done so much for me already. You have saved my life. I will not have you jeopardize your own."

"And I shall not have you risking yours!" Twin spots of red flamed Audrey's cheeks, her friend's temper fueled by love and concern.

Catherine gave Audrey's hands a tight squeeze before releasing them to sit back in her chair, exhaling a slow breath. "Jane will not survive Simon's cruelty; that much is certain. And I simply cannot let it happen."

"Catherine, if you make your whereabouts known Simon shall have you hanged for murder. How is that helping Jane?"

"But that's just it. If I could only learn whatever

forced John and Simon to flee London, it may just give me the upper hand I need. Perhaps whatever chased them out of here could be used against him to prevent his marriage."

Audrey sipped her tea, thoughtful. "This could be a way to rid yourself of him for good."

Catherine sat pole stiff in her chair, determination flooding her veins. "I see it rather as a chance to do something right. Something I perhaps should have done years ago."

"Confronting him, you mean?"

"Yes." She pressed her lips tight in a thin line of resolve. "If I say nothing, and he marries Jane Denbigh, she'll be fettered to a foul-mouthed wife beater just as I was. I cannot do that, Audrey. I won't gain my freedom from Simon through another girl's descent into hell."

Audrey nodded. "'Tis no surprise you feel that way. You are not one to benefit on the back of someone else's misery." She nibbled on a bite of almond cake and sat back in her chair, considering. "Will you say anything to Miles?"

"How can I?" Melancholy shadowed Catherine's quiet reply. "He knows nothing of my previous life." *As I know nothing of his.*

"I see."

"Do you...is there something wrong with staying quiet?" Catherine frowned. What could her friend be hinting at? "'Tis the right decision to keep this from him, Audrey. You know it is."

"If you feel that way, then of course it is." She sipped more tea, ate more cake, her words taking root in Catherine's mind.

"But it must be this way. Is it not so?" Catherine

leaned forward in her chair, hands clasped together as though pleading for assurance that she was doing the right thing. "This...relationship I have with Miles. It is physical only, just as the others. No emotions. None at all."

"Are you telling me, or are you trying to convince yourself?"

So unsettled she could not sit, Catherine shot once more to her feet. Audrey was all but forcing her to admit something she'd rather keep hidden. But despite her best efforts the truth kept coming at her, clawing its way above ground no matter how hard she tried to bury it. She knew she could deny it no more.

"I love him, Audrey."

Audrey rose, too, and put her arms around Catherine. "I know," she said, pulling her close.

Catherine trembled in Audrey's arms, so afraid of loving again after what had happened with John, yet helpless to stop it.

"Do not fret so, Catherine. There's nothing wrong with loving him."

Dear, kind Audrey. Catherine's pillar of strength during her marriage to John and even more so afterward once she'd escaped. She'd transformed Catherine, helping her evolve into the person she was today. And now once again Audrey stood by Catherine's side, softly nudging her to admit something she was afraid of and helping her figure out what to do.

Catherine dashed away a lone tear trailing down her cheek before pulling away. A spark of determination stiffened her spine. "'Tis time Miles knows the truth, though I fear I shall lose him."

"There is naught to fear. If Miles Hawkins is

worthy of you, he'll understand. Besides, it's possible he may be able to help. He's lived here all his life and is well connected. Perhaps he even knows something of the scandal, or is acquainted with someone who does."

They strolled toward the door. There was still so much she didn't know about Miles, and she could not be certain he'd ever want to tell her more. But if there was any chance of a future with him, she must confront her past and tell him the truth.

****

Catherine peered into the looking glass at her vanity. Her skin was sallow, her eyes tinged red. Sleep last eve had been naught but a fanciful wish. She knew she had to tell Miles the truth about her past, yet the thought of actually doing so tormented her.

A knock on the door shook away her reverie. Rosy cheeked Hannah peeked through the doorway. "Lord Miles for you, miss."

A shiver of fear stole through Catherine's heart, but she hid it well. "Very good," she replied. "Inform him I shall be down momentarily."

As the young maid whisked away, Catherine smoothed her gown and inhaled a calming breath. Her fingers had grown cold, matching the chill of trepidation in her heart. She was doing the right thing, but knowing it made it no less difficult.

As she entered the sitting room where Miles awaited, he turned and walked toward her but stopped short of taking her into his arms. She could only surmise that her face projected her somber state.

"You are well?" he asked, his eyes reflecting concern.

"I am, yes." She gestured to two upholstered

armchairs, angled so those sitting in them would face one another.

"Please," she invited, her extended arm gesturing to the chairs. As they took their seats she expelled a deep breath. "Thank you for coming."

"You know I will. Always."

"I wanted to talk to you...about that note."

"It is not necessary. As I told you, I understand about secrets."

"I know you do. But there are things I must tell you."

Moist sweat dampened her chilly palms. Catherine balled her fingers into fists and licked her lips. Were the moment not so important she may have laughed, for she felt as nervous as a young scullery maid before receiving her first kiss.

"The message I received yesterday, the one from Audrey. It—" Her heart slammed against her chest, and the roar of blood in her ears whooshed as loud as pouring rain. Catherine looked straight at Miles, into his dark, fathomless eyes, and willed herself to speak. "It was about Simon Underhill."

Miles said nothing.

"He's the brother of...of John Underhill. My husband."

She waited for a reaction from him, anything that would tell her what he was thinking, or feeling, but his face remained as expressionless as stone. A small twitch fluttered in the back of his jaw but no more, nothing that would indicate whether he felt surprise, or fury, or anything at all. For a moment, she wanted to give him a hard shove, or douse him with a bucket of icy water, anything to force some kind of reaction.

A dark thought flitted through her mind. Perhaps Miles was angry, so angry he was speechless. Her stomach clenched with a sick knot of fear. Could that be it? She hoped she was wrong, but his silence didn't bode well.

She released a shaky breath. "I haven't seen him for over four years, not since the day I left him."

At last Miles found his voice. "Why did you leave?"

"I..." She hesitated. Even after so many years, speaking of John still nauseated her, the very thought of him like toxic bile.

But she pressed on, determined Miles should know everything. "John beat me. I allowed it to continue for two years after we were married, for I thought surely it would stop if I could simply be a better wife. 'Twas Audrey who told me early on in the marriage that I should leave John. If only it had not taken two years before I believed her."

His expression softened as concern flickered in his eyes. "But what of your family? Why have they not told John of your whereabouts? Surely your leaving him has caused quite a scandal."

Catherine tamped down the knife-wrenching pain in her heart that came whenever she thought of her family.

"They never knew where I went." Her voice was little more than a whisper. "I didn't contact them after I left. If they'd known my whereabouts, they would have done everything in their power to force my return. No matter what sort of man a woman marries, they would not have believed anything so horrid justifies leaving. So 'twas not possible for them to know where I went."

"You speak of them in the past," Miles noted quietly.

"Yes." Catherine nodded. "In the years since I fled, they have both passed. I have no other family."

"So Audrey never told them?"

"Audrey does not know them."

Miles' brow wrinkled in confusion. "I thought she was your aunt."

"No. That is a story of pure invention. In truth, Audrey is a distant cousin of John and Simon's, so she and I are related only through marriage. When I escaped, it was Audrey who saved me. I arrived at her home in the middle of the night after John had tried to force his way on me. That very evening she and I devised a plan that would enable me to transform myself from Lucy Underhill to Catherine Sheffield. I have never once looked back."

"Nor should you. A man such as that doesn't deserve to call you wife." He expelled a breath, his fingers balled in a tight grip where they rested in his lap. Anger vibrated from his body.

"The night I left John," she continued, "we had quarreled. He...he'd spent most of the evening in an alehouse and was drunk as a sow's ear by the time he returned. He'd decided he wanted me, but I would have none of it. I refused him, something I'd not done before. He became enraged and insisted I perform as wife. But I would not."

She felt the sting of tears in her eyes, but they would be denied. Never again would she cry over that wretched John Underhill. Furiously, she blinked them back.

"We struggled in my bedchamber, and I managed

to get away. Just as I reached the door, I looked back and saw him shove off the bed and take steps toward me. I was horrified, thinking my chance at escape was gone. But fortune shone upon me that night, though it seems dreadful to say so."

Miles narrowed his eyes, confused. "What do you mean?"

"John became entangled in his own breeches and fell. His head struck the fireplace mantel and then the floor and..." She shoved aside the memory of all that blood as her voice dropped to a whisper. "He died."

The room fell silent as Miles digested her words. She wished his expression would divulge how he felt about all she'd just told him, but he remained guarded as a fortress, revealing nothing.

At last she took a breath and continued, spelling out the rest of the story about Simon's arrival and how she and Mrs. Tuckett hid John's body before Simon discovered his brother was dead. She spoke of drugging Simon and of her nighttime escape to Audrey, and she let Miles know how Audrey maintained distant contact with her relations, enough for them to know the talk about town.

"Simon believes I murdered his brother," she finished. "And he wants revenge. If he ever finds me he will see me hang for murder."

"That shall never happen." His voice was hard as a blade and Catherine's heart fluttered, as if a medieval knight sat before her.

"I, too, vowed Simon would never find me. But—" She swallowed back her fear as she thought of Jane Denbigh. "The note from Audrey changed that."

"What do you mean?" He leaned forward in his

chair, his jaw tense. "Catherine, no matter what, you cannot let him know where you are."

"I have to."

"You do not. I can help—"

"Miles, please." She held up her hands, palms out. "Please, listen to me. 'Tis possible you may be able to help, but first I must tell you everything."

He remained in place, his gaze fused to hers, but he nodded and waited for her to go on.

She told the rest of the story, telling him of her love and friendship with Jane and of the horrid news that Simon planned to marry her. She also spoke of the conversation she'd had with Audrey and gossip of the scandal that had driven Simon and John Underhill from London.

"Yet we don't know what it is," she admitted as her story ended. "And I thought perhaps, since you are so well connected, you may know something of it?"

With seeming reluctance he slowly shook his head. "I do not," he admitted, exhaling a long breath. "I bloody well wish I did, but neither their names nor talk of gossip concerning them has made its way to me."

A cloud of disappointment choked the room into silence. Catherine sank in her chair, the crush of hope heavy in her breast. Still, she would not admit defeat.

"Is it possible you know of someone who would have knowledge of the scandal?"

His brows furrowed, a look of concentration etched his forehead. His gaze was faraway, cast toward the window, but Catherine guessed his focus was not on the scenery outdoors.

"I don't believe I..." He shifted his attention toward Catherine and his eyes lit with an excited glow.

"You've remembered something?"

"Yes." Miles nodded. "I believe I have, in fact. There's a woman I know of whose business, for a steep price, makes her very well...ah, *acquainted*...with gentlemen about town." He glanced down at the floor, having the decency to look embarrassed. "Apologies, Catherine. I don't mean to be vulgar. But you understand my meaning?"

"No apology necessary. And yes, I understand." She couldn't deny the shards of jealousy needling her heart as she wondered whether Miles had first-hand knowledge of the harlot, but she forcefully set it aside. Her focus had to remain on stopping Simon.

"It was your friend, Clifton, who told me about Miss Felicity Penworth. 'Twas he who once mentioned her during a conversation at Tom's."

"Did he? Why?"

Miles waved off the question. "It matters not, truly. But 'tis possible Miss Penworth may have the information you seek. She's well-connected and knows a great many people. And from what I've heard, has lived in London all her life."

Catherine's heartbeat skipped with a thread of hope. "I must speak with her. Could you help me arrange it?"

Miles leaned forward and took hold of her trembling fingers. Warmth from his hands flowed soothingly into hers like beams of sunlight. His dark eyes traveled the length of her before locking with her gaze.

"You are an incredibly brave woman, Catherine Sheffield," he said softly. "And unlike anyone I have ever known. Of course I'll help you."

An unexpected stir of desire wove through the air like sinuous wisps of smoke. Catherine's mouth went dry as Miles rose from his chair and tucked his hands beneath her arms, guiding her to stand before him. Then, with a touch as soft as a whisper, he cupped her face, his thumbs gently caressing her cheeks as he drew her into his kiss.

His warm mouth possessed hers, and she melted into him. Emotion swirled like butterflies in her head. As much as she tried denying it, she was falling deeper and deeper under Miles' magnetic spell. She treaded dangerous waters, ones she'd ruthlessly avoided since her flight from hell four years ago.

But as his lips lingered against hers before he deepened the kiss and slipped his tongue into her mouth, Catherine knew she was perilously close to allowing Miles Hawkins be the exception to her steadfast rule. She eased away before the kiss took over and evolved into passion neither could resist.

Letting out a calming breath, she stepped back to put some distance between them and allow her thundering heartbeat to calm.

"I want—"

"You don't need to explain," Miles stopped her. "I want you as well. But right now the focus is on stopping Simon. Once that has happened..." He trailed a finger down her arm, a sizzling indication of what the future held.

They walked together to the door and waited while Hannah fetched his hat. After she'd done so and he prepared to depart, he took Catherine's hands in his.

"I shall do whatever it takes to find Felicity Penworth," he promised, "and arrange a meeting. But remember, she may not have the information you seek." Concern in his sable eyes reflected back at her.

She smiled and withdrew one hand to stroke her fingertips along his chiseled jaw. "I am prepared for disappointment," she assured him. "But I must at least try."

"Of course you must." He brushed a last kiss across her lips and opened the door. "You shall hear from me just as soon as possible." With a polite tip of his hat he left, leaving behind a trail of hope in his wake.

****

A patter of rain, like pebbles, beat softly against the roof of Catherine's carriage. She glanced out the window at the park, bereft of visitors now that twilight approached. She'd had her driver, Henry, pull the coach to a stop in an isolated area at the far end of the park. It was here where she awaited her visitor.

Minutes later she caught the distant thud of horses' hooves against the cobbled streets. Steadily the sound grew louder until the carriage came to a halt close to Catherine's. She saw Henry jump down from his perch and open the carriage door. A fashionably dressed woman emerged, carrying herself with confidence. Her footsteps were sure as she approached Catherine's coach.

"Miss Penworth?" Henry posed the question.

"Indeed I am."

"Then I'm pleased to welcome you, miss."

He opened the door and grasped the woman's hand to assist her as she stepped up the stairs and into Catherine's coach.

She settled onto the opposite seat. Her dress was an

exorbitantly expensive silk, but the well-made garment lacked decorum. Excessive lace and ruffle only barely muted the blinding yellow color. The courtesan kept her hair styled high and topped it with a feathered hat. She dressed the part of a well-to-do woman, but her true nature sat not far below the gilded surface. Like a caged animal threatening to bite anyone who came too close, an air of suspicion surrounded her.

"Thank you for meeting me, Miss Penworth," Catherine began. "I recognize the circumstances are perhaps a bit unusual."

"That they are, Miss Sheffield. Can't say I would have come if it weren't for Lord Clifton. But he seems to set great store by you, so..." She shrugged. "What are you wanting from me?"

"Information."

"Who says I have it?"

"You may well not. But I would like to at least ask." Catherine smoothed her palms along her skirts and expelled a deep breath. "I understand you are well acquainted with a great number of people in London."

"I know a few."

"I'm told you've lived here for many years."

She crossed her arms in front of her and pinned Catherine with a stare. "And if I have?"

Catherine withheld a sigh of frustration. She wasn't going to get anywhere if this woman remained so closely guarded. She decided on a different tactic.

"Felicity, may I be frank with you?"

The courtesan sat back, extending the distance between herself and Catherine. She nodded.

"As is the case with many people, there are things in my life I wish to remain secret."

125

Skepticism narrowed the other woman's eyes, but Catherine's honesty at least appeared to have captured her attention.

"In order for me to do that," Catherine continued, "I need some information. This is where you may be able to help."

"Mayhap." Felicity shrugged. "But barring no disrespect, why should I?"

"For the simple reason that you are a woman. A woman who's had, I would imagine, to toil more than most in this life. Who hasn't necessarily had an easy time of things. Who understands that doing a favor now may reap a *very* lucrative reward in the future." She expelled a soft breath. "It is for those reasons I am very much hoping you will help me."

Catherine leaned forward in her seat and trapped Felicity's gaze in her own, refusing to let go. Felicity moved her head in a barely perceptible nod. "Very well, miss. I'll help you if I can."

Relieved she'd secured the woman's agreement, Catherine allowed herself to partially relax against the velvet seat of her carriage. "I'm looking for information on someone who used to live in London several years ago."

The courtesan raised a well plucked brow. "What's the name of this someone?"

"Underhill. John or Simon. I want to know anything you can tell me on either or both of them. Anything."

For a moment Felicity said nothing, but she balled her hands into tight fists as her lips slowly twisted in a bitter grimace. "I know those two all right," she spat out, her voice hard as stone. "And as far as I'm concerned there's a place in hell for them both."

Excitement surged through Catherine's blood and she stopped herself just in time from gasping aloud. Felicity's cold statement was all the proof she needed that the courtesan spoke of none other than Catherine's dead husband and his brother.

She tightened her folded hands in her lap and leaned toward Felicity, her sharp gaze locked to the other woman. "Tell me everything you know."

****

Miles stretched his long legs before him in the chaise lounge chair, peering at Catherine with a smile of satisfaction gracing his handsome face.

"I'm glad Miss Penworth was able to help."

"As am I." Catherine reached out a hand toward him, basking in the tender sensation of him clasping her fingers in his warm grip.

"Thank you again for everything you've done. I hope you know how much it means to me."

"I appreciate the kind words, Catherine, but they are not necessary." His voice dropped as he caressed the back of her hand with his thumb. "There's nothing I wouldn't do for you."

His kindness brought a surge of unexpected emotion and she reminded herself this wasn't supposed to happen. No feelings toward a man—ever. That had been her vow for the past four years and it had worked. Except then Miles had come along...

Seemingly unaware of where her thoughts had strayed, Miles sat back in his chair and templed his fingers beneath his chain. "We should discuss what comes next," he said, shifting the conversation's tone. "Where and how Simon will be confronted."

Her posture stiffened and she sat up in her chair. "I must make haste if I'm to prevent this wedding. My bags have been packed and the carriage is prepared. I leave on the morrow."

"*You* leave on the morrow?" His dark eyes took on a sudden glint. "What are you talking about, Catherine? Are you mad? You cannot possibly intend to make this journey alone."

"Of course not. My driver shall take me."

"Your *driver*?"

She flinched at his harsh tone but told herself his agitation came from concern. Still, his raised voice stirred within her a pot of fearful memories, ones she needed to bury once and for all. She grasped the chair's arm until her knuckles whitened.

"Yes, Miles." Her voice was firm. "My driver, Henry. You don't know him, but he's strong as an ox; he shall serve as my protector as well."

His brows knit with confusion. "I cannot allow you to travel all that way, Catherine. You must know I'm intending to accompany you. 'Tis a lengthy journey."

"I know very well how long it is. I made it once before."

"But—"

"There is no discussion. This is something I need to do on my own."

His mouth clapped shut, and Catherine relaxed marginally in the chair. Her decisive tone had quelled Miles' argument—for the moment.

Expelling a deep breath, she continued, "The night I left was the most difficult of my life. I'd never done anything like it before. I was so scared, and felt so alone. The only person in the world I knew I could trust was Audrey, and as I've told you, she saved me."

"She's an extraordinary woman."

She smiled. "Audrey was my protector as well as my mentor. One of the many things she taught me was independence, which was important, because I never knew how to be me. I needed to discover the kind of person I was so I could begin living as myself, as Catherine Sheffield, and not just as someone's wife, or daughter, or sister."

Admiration for what she'd gone through shone in his eyes. "I would imagine it took a lot of courage."

"It did. Some of Audrey's teachings were difficult, but necessary."

"Such as?"

She paused before answering, balling suddenly trembling fingers into fists. "Such as distancing myself from the influences of others so I could make my own decisions."

She watched Miles closely, gauging his reaction. She may as well have studied a rock. He revealed nothing, neither in his gaze nor posture nor lack of words. His expression was smooth as a freshly ironed sheet. But she'd begun to learn his quiet ways, and she knew for all the tranquility he projected on the outside, inside his mind whirred like so many wheels and cogs.

At last he said quietly, "I assume you refer to emotional distance. So you are not unduly influenced."

"Yes." She nodded. "Especially with...with men." The burn of blush heated her cheeks, but she pressed on. "Audrey is unconventional, some say too much. But 'twas she who taught me a woman can enjoy physical pleasure for its own sake without risking the pain and heartache of an emotional entanglement. Yet indulging in such relationships requires me to be mindful of keeping distance and maintaining my independence."

"Such as driving yourself to engagements."

"Yes." She nodded. "A small but necessary requirement. But above all else..." Her tone wavered. "Above all else I vowed never again to develop feelings for any man. To do so would be to lose myself, and I must still be me. So if I sense feelings beginning to emerge—whether mine or his—I immediately break any ties between us."

She stopped, pulse racing, wishing she could compel Miles to understand. Surely he must. He himself held secrets he chose not to share. He, too, maintained emotional distance. 'Tis why their relationship worked—for both of them.

But instead of hearing him respond with words of reassurance, she sensed a noticeable shift in the air.

Miles' posture changed, becoming closed in, as if warding off blows. He cleared his throat and rose from the chair. "Thank you for speaking with me, Catherine. I now understand why you wish to journey alone and I shall not stop you." His voice was formal, wooden, like he was concealing some emotion roiling just beneath the surface.

"Please send word once you've arrived home, if only so I will know you are safe. It is a long journey." Then, with a stiff bow, Miles turned on his heel and headed for the door.

No! Catherine silently cried out, her mind a whirl of emotions spinning like a top. This was all wrong. It was not what she wanted. She had so much more to say.

The words she'd intended to speak were screaming behind her lips, begging for release so she could tell him how she felt. How for the past four years she'd never allowed emotional attachment to any man until he came along and changed all her rules. It was why she needed to confront the fears of her past alone in order to find strength to move forward with her future. And how she wanted that future to include him.

But, yet. Was it wise to tell him so? The way he'd reacted gave her pause. He had his own secrets. Perhaps they would prohibit their relationship. Perhaps her saying anything more would be utterly without meaning.

He reached the doorway and grasped the handle. He paused, just for a moment, as if allowing Catherine one last chance to say something—anything—to stop him from leaving. But she could not utter the words. The only sound in the room was a soft, ragged gasp as if torn from her heart.

Then Miles was gone, leaving behind the faintest whisper of himself, a trace of scent elusive as it was fragile. Before Catherine had time to breathe in the smell of him and capture that last bit of essence it, too, had vanished, and she was left with nothing.

****

Miles welcomed the bracing slap of air against his face. He leaned hard on his stallion, urging him faster as they roared along the dirt road. He pulled on the reins to turn them north, reveling in the effort required to control his mount. He needed to expel his pent up fury on something, and a half ton of unruly beast was a perfect match.

He cursed as he thought back to the conversation he'd just had with Catherine. He was such a fool! Now everything the Earl of Clifton told him at the coffeehouse made perfect sense. The man had alluded to the fact his relationship with Catherine was a thing of the past, but that must have happened because the earl had developed feelings for her that were not returned. What a sorry piece of dung Clifton was. It was obvious he coveted the position Miles now held. No wonder the man had been insufferable.

Miles' heart stung with wretched disappointment. He was in no better position than Clifton. Only moments ago Catherine had informed him she would take her upcoming journey alone. His company was unwanted and now he knew why.

Despite his personal vow, he had tentatively begun to believe he was willing to take a chance on loving again. He'd said nothing to Catherine, of course, not wanting to push her, needing to be sure she could accept what he offered. As it turned out, she could not. It was obvious she'd sensed his feelings, perhaps even before he did so himself. So she was doing to him what she did with all others when feelings began to sprout. She was saying goodbye.

He cursed his stupidity. Was he such a dolt to have forgotten the searing agony from having what he loved torn apart like a limb from his body? Apparently so, he thought with a bitter grimace, for despite his determination against such a thing ever happening, Catherine had bewitched him. He knew he was on the verge of loving once again. And just as before, it was about to be taken away.

He tensed, every muscle granite-hard as he braced for the black clouds that forever invaded his mind when he let in memories of the past. He pulled the reins and stopped his mount near a quiet brook. Jumping down, he led the horse to drink and sat on a rock near the water's edge. For the first time in months, his mind drifted back to Anne.

What a different person he'd been back then, before life's tragedies cast a shadow over everything he'd known to be pure and good. Prior to his world crashing down around him, life had been a bounteous feast of possibility. He'd known love, and he'd known happiness. The fragility of those emotions, how easily they could be destroyed, was as unheard of as walking on stars. Everything had been so easy back then. Life's path was smooth, without obstacles. Until...until...

He closed his eyes and awaited the blinding pain of his past to arrow into his heart. Pain so fierce and sharp he could scarcely draw breath. Except...it didn't come.

Where was it? Why was he able, this time, to think of Anne and not be hurled into a black abyss of tragedy? Could it be because a healing balm had finally begun soothing those deep wounds? A balm in the form of a wickedly smart, fiercely independent and breathtakingly beautiful woman named Catherine? A woman with the power to mend his broken heart?

A whinny from his mount distracted his thoughts. Miles grasped a few stones from the ground and stood, then one by one skipped the stones across the quiet brook.

His mind returned to Catherine. She didn't want emotional attachment; neither did he. Theirs a relationship of physical love only. It was what they both desired. No courting, no complications, and when it was over the ending was quick and tidy. Except that arrangement was beginning to unravel. What they thought they'd wanted had changed, at least it had for him.

He frowned. Perhaps this wasn't the road he and Catherine had planned to travel, but they'd been set upon its path nonetheless. Insight seized him and at once his decision was made. His lips pressed tight in a grim line of determination. He couldn't know what was in Catherine's mind, but for himself—and perhaps for the both of them—he knew what he had to do.

****

The clopping of the horses' hooves were as dull as Catherine's thoughts. She dropped her head against the carriage back and closed her eyes, overcome by exhaustion. She'd spent a sleepless night reliving the conversation with Miles and trying in vain to tell herself his departure was for the best, knowing all along it was a lie.

Like it or not, she was in love with him. What cruel irony that the one time she actually wanted a man to stay, he had decided it was better to leave.

Suddenly she jerked awake, startled by outside commotion. She heard the frightened whinny of her horses and the commands of her driver as he tried to calm them. An angry voice joined the chorus, and she knew at once to whom it belonged.

She stuck her head out the carriage window to see what was afoot. Breathing heavily, hair windswept and disheveled, his eyes shadowed by a lack of sleep, Miles sat atop his horse, blocking the path.

"Be off with you!" Catherine's driver, Henry, shouted.

"Not before I see her."

"You'll more likely see my fist down your throat!" Henry balled his huge hands and waved them threateningly before Miles when Catherine called a halt to the pending dual.

"'Tis all right, Henry," she assured him, nodding toward Miles. "I know this man."

The driver was at once contrite. "I beg forgiveness, Miss Catherine," he said. "I thought he meant to harm you. I did not know—"

"Of course you did not. But perhaps you could take this gentleman's horse to the nearby stream and water him while Lord Miles and I speak for a moment in my carriage."

"Certainly. Whatever you wish."

Miles dismounted and handed the reins over to the driver, then climbed into the carriage and took a seat beside Catherine.

His face was deluged with signs of sleeplessness. Lines of strain etched the corners of his mouth. His dark eyes were sunken and bloodshot, with small, puffy bags protruding beneath the lower lids. Tangled locks of hair jutted in all directions. But despite his appearance and wild ride he seemed calmer than he'd been the night before. It was as though he had come to a decision that lifted a monumental burden from his shoulders.

"I apologize for appearing so suddenly," he began, reaching out to grasp her hands in his, "but it was imperative I reach you before you'd gone too far."

"What is it, Miles? Has something happened?"

"Yes." He nodded. "I realized I cannot let you go."

"But—"

"Please. Let me finish." He held up a hand as though to bar her words and expelled a ragged breath. "I thought of you all night, Catherine. Try as I might, I couldn't get you out of my mind."

"'Twas the same with me," she admitted softly, a ray of hope lifting her spirits.

"Then you know as well as I why it is. There's a connection between us, Catherine. You feel it as do I, and I'm speaking not only of our physical attraction to one another but of our emotional decisions. Past experience has made us both determined to keep our hearts closed."

She nodded while looking deep into his eyes, remembering the shadow of pain she frequently saw there.

"I thought at first 'twas a good thing you keep yourself detached," he continued, "for I, too, do the same. I even tried supporting your decision to confront Simon alone, for I understood the need to maintain your independence."

He slid closer on the bench of the carriage and held her face between his warm, strong hands. His thumbs stroked her cheeks, then he brought his lips to hers and kissed her so tenderly she thought her heart would break.

"But I cannot support that decision any longer," he whispered when they parted. "Like it or not, I am a part of your life, Catherine. Your life right now and hopefully your life in the future."

Her breath stuck fast in her throat as she stared into his eyes. Could it be? Was he saying...

"If you are not freed from the hauntings of your past you can never be free to have a future with me."

For a moment Catherine felt as though her heartbeat was suspended in time and she had to, simply *had* to keep it that way because if she moved, or breathed, or blinked her eyes she would destroy this moment forever and would never again know the pure, unequivocal joy of hearing that the man she was falling in love with wanted to be with her.

"I know this is not what you want, Catherine," Miles continued, "but maybe—"

She let out a small cry as her eyes filled with tears. For a moment she couldn't speak around the boulder lodged in her throat, tears of elation rolling down her cheeks.

It was likely Miles mistook her silence for reluctance, for he dropped his hands from her face and put distance between them. But as he attempted to slide away Catherine's slim fingers gripped his arm and held him fast. "Do not leave and ruin the happiest moment of my life."

Tears continued to trickle down her cheeks, but she smiled through them, her heart swelling with emotion. "I want you in my life, Miles," she whispered. "I want it so much I couldn't tell you because I could not bear to lose you. I thought if you knew how I felt it would drive you away, and I would rather have you with me and keep my feelings hidden than take the risk of never seeing you again."

"My sweet," he murmured, drawing her into his arms. "I feel just the same. I didn't want to ruin what we had together. But last night I realized I could not keep silent. Even if you rejected what I offered I was willing to take the chance, because I do not want to lose you."

His words swept in and gave wing to her heart, lifting her fears about loving once more. She'd ruthlessly vowed it would never happen again but yet it was, and nothing felt more right. Miles had not yet voiced his words of love to her, but she allowed herself to believe that one day soon he might. Her entire body trembled, flooded by a wellspring of joy.

"I want to go with you," he continued. "You will face Simon alone as you wish, but I will be there, right outside, for your protection. I need to be sure you're safe."

She closed her eyes as she rested her head against his chest, feeling his heartbeat vibrating against her cheek, the warmth of his body flowing into her blood.

"Yes," she whispered, not just in response to what Miles had said but also to acknowledge the harmonious perfection of the moment. They were two souls united, afraid of making promises but more fearful still not to try. Catherine knew together they would defeat whatever fell their way, whether it was Simon's vileness or the tortured hauntings of Miles' past. Their strength together would prove invincible.

Chapter Six

The heavy oak door swung open, and the butler's face drained of color. "Lucy!"

"No, Smithens." Catherine swept past the open-mouthed man and into her former home with unshakable fortitude. "Lucy Underhill is no more. Please inform Simon that Miss Catherine Sheffield has come to call."

The butler's eyebrows wrinkled in confusion. "Catherine...Sheffield?"

"If you please, Mr. Smithens. And do make haste for I haven't much time."

"Certainly, Miss Sheffield." Although likely brimming with questions, the butler quickly regained his usual stoicism and left to do her bidding.

Catherine stood alone in the sitting room. Everything was essentially the same as when she had left it. The furniture, the paintings, the wall decorations, all were selections she had made while in the youthful bloom of married life. How she had wanted to please John at that time, eager to prove her worthiness to a wealthy, titled landowner. She never could have dreamed he would turn out to be such a colossal fiend.

Strolling over to the window, she drew aside the heavy brocade drapery and gazed outside, smiling as she saw her carriage move into place. She took a deep breath while reaching for the hidden pocket sewn into her skirts. Her fingers stroked the smooth agate haft of the pen knife tucked away, drawing strength from knowing it was there if she needed it.

Footsteps in the hall—the heavy, unmistakable thumpings of Simon—interrupted her musings. Just as well. She was ready to confront him and be on her way, this time for good.

"Miss Sheffield," he said, stepping into the room.

He had his hand extended, ready to greet his unknown guest, when he caught sight of Catherine, and every movement stopped as if he'd suddenly turned to ice. His mouth stayed open, his arm froze in the air. For the first time since Catherine had known him, Simon Underhill was speechless.

It didn't last long. Once he recognized the elegant woman standing in his home as the one he believed had murdered his brother, the shock melted away and was replaced with a satisfied, evil grin. He folded his arms across his chest.

"So," he sneered, looking her up and down as though assessing the prospects in a whorehouse. "Look what the cat dragged in."

"Not for long." Catherine ordered herself to steady her voice. Though her convictions remained as solid as ever, now that she actually faced Simon, knowledge of his violent ways seeped like poison into her pores, eating away her resolve. She focused on Miles, on his support and his strength, and it gave her the antidote she needed to go on.

She took a step toward Simon. "I am here only long enough to inform you that you will not be marrying Jane Denbigh."

"Indeed?" He snorted. "And who's going to stop

me? You?" He threw his head back with a malicious laugh. "You must be joking, Lucy."

"I assure you, I am not," Catherine replied. "And as I have informed you, Lucy is no more. My name is Catherine Sheffield."

"Your name is Lucy Underhill, you murderess bitch!" Blotches of red splashed Simon's cheeks and his eyes popped from his head as he abandoned all earlier sense of amusement. Shades of his violent temper sprang forth.

"Now you listen to me, Lucy," he hissed, moving closer to her and shaking his giant fist, "and you listen well. For four years my brother has turned cold in his grave, and I've been tormented every day since, knowing I allowed his murderer to flee. I vowed revenge, and revenge I shall have."

Drops of spittle flew from his lips as he thundered at her, his voice rising as his temper grew. "You killed him, you filthy whore, and for what you did I'll see you hanged and thrown in a grave where maggots can dine on your rotting flesh."

He grabbed her upper arm, trapping her where she stood. "But before that happens, I'll get what was coming to me all those years ago—a nice fuck from John's former wench." Leaning in toward her, his tongue snaked out and swiped the side of her throat, leaving her skin coated with a wet trail of saliva.

Reeling with disgust, Catherine whirled, breaking Simon's grip on her arm. She sprang back, putting enough distance between herself and Simon so he could not reach her. "Touch me again," she snarled, her voice dripping daggers, "and I will claw your eyes out."

Physically Simon was far stronger, but

determination fueled Catherine, fierce as a she-wolf with newborn cubs. Confusion clouded his gaze and he dropped his hand to his side.

"Get back here," he said, though with far less menace than moments ago. "Don't think for a minute you're getting away from me."

"Not only will I be getting away from you," Catherine replied, squaring her shoulders and refusing to back down. "But 'tis I, not you, who shall have revenge."

Her statement seemed to have momentarily surprised him. He narrowed his eyes. "What are you talking about?"

Seizing her advantage, Catherine calmly replied, "Does the name Felicity Penworth mean anything to you?"

She basked in the delicious satisfaction of taking Simon Underhill unawares. He dropped his gaze, his eyes shifting to and fro. For a moment he even turned away, likely an attempt to mask his astonishment over Catherine knowing Felicity's name. But know it she did, and she used that knowledge for all it was worth.

With confidence she'd never before felt in front of her former husband's vicious younger brother, Catherine faced him head on. "It seems you and your brother amassed quite a gambling debt back when you used to live in London, isn't that right?"

"What do you know of—"

"You owe thousands and thousands of pounds to several people. Several *very important* people who would love to learn what happened to you."

She waited with unconcealed satisfaction as the color on Simon's face grew steadily beet red. His eyes narrowed into hard, angry slits, but the woman Catherine had become didn't fear his vile temper as Lucy Underhill would have. Instead, she savored it.

"Miss Penworth seems *intimately* acquainted with you, Simon. John as well. Of course, 'tis because she was, in the literal sense, intimately acquainted with you."

"Now, you listen to me, Lucy, I—"

"It's *Catherine*. I shall not tell you once more. Get it through your thick skull, Simon. You do not lord over me as your brother once did." She took a step toward him, heart thundering in her chest as fury from years of living with fear and abuse coursed through her veins and incited her courage. "Felicity Penworth knows the names of the people you and John cheated before setting loose for the countryside. She has proof as well. Papers, official records, notes in yours and John's handwriting."

"Why, you..." His voice was a growl, as if to sound severe and threatening, warning her to stop.

"What, Simon?" Catherine merely plucked a stray piece of lint from the sleeve of her gown, no more afraid of him than she was of the lint. "Did you think Miss Penworth was not smart enough to read? Not clever enough to realize all the papers you and John left so carelessly strewn about in the flat where you kept her would one day be invaluable to her? That was a big mistake. Just one of many. Not only did she save loads of incriminating evidence on the two of you, but she kept in her heart the ruthless fury of a woman scorned."

"Scorned? She was a whore—"

"Silence!" She held a hand before his face, effectively stopping his words. "Your derision is

143

unwelcome, both by me and by Miss Penworth. Who, I might add, prefers to think of herself as a woman of commerce."

Confusion puckered Simon's face. His brows knit; his lips were pressed tight. "Commerce?"

"She's a rather well-to-do woman nowadays. Not that you had any hand in it after throwing her to the streets right before you fled." She welcomed the anger coating her words. Her fingers curled into fists as she paced before Simon.

"For two long years, Felicity Penworth had no home. She lived with cold and rain and the constant fear only a woman living alone on the wretched streets of London would know. And it's all because of you and John and your ruthless treatment of her."

She moved in to seal his fate, standing directly before him like a viper ready to strike. "Felicity Penworth would love nothing more than to see you spend your final days in the hell of debtor's prison. And if you marry Jane Denbigh, that's exactly where you'll be. I'll tell her and everyone else exactly what became of you and how to find you."

"You dare not!"

"I more than dare, Simon, I will most certainly do it." Catherine's voice turned as hard as flint. "And don't think your status will save you. Members of the nobility like being cheated even less than common folk. It embarrasses them, makes them angry. There's not a single person around who would stick his neck out to save your wretched hide."

He recoiled, actually took a step backward, proof that her words were affecting him as she'd hoped. Simon was afraid. She could tell by his rounded eyes and shallow breaths. And that fear, cold and slimy and unwanted as a snake, was slithering its way into his mind.

"What madness is this?" he breathed.

"Madness? Whatever do you mean?"

He nervously cleared his throat and went on. "Why should you care of Jane Denbigh?"

"Because I was once that girl," she replied. "Naïve and innocent, thinking your brother actually loved me. But he was doing exactly what you are attempting with Jane—hiding your vile reputation behind the pure goodness of a young girl. You care nothing for Jane and will discard her as easily as you discarded Felicity Penworth. But I am here to tell you, it will never happen. Not with her, nor with anyone else."

"You bitch," Simon blustered, puffing out his chest to exert authority. "You cannot stop me if you're swinging from a noose. You murdered my brother, and I'll see you hanged."

Catherine chose not to point out that Simon's last statement sounded far more like a point of negotiation than a threat. Instead, buoyed by the certainty she had him exactly where she wanted him, she stated in a quiet voice, "I most certainly can stop you, and I most certainly will. I didn't murder John and you have no proof of it. But I have proof of your debts and plenty of it. So if you wish not to see the inside of a filthy jail cell, here are my terms."

She counted them off on her fingers as Simon quaked. "First, if you try to marry Jane, or indeed any other girl, I will make your whereabouts known to everyone in London and you go to jail.

"Second, you will pay twenty thousand pounds to

Felicity Penworth. 'Tis small compensation for the misery you put her through, but better than nothing. In exchange, she has agreed to keep what she knows to herself."

Simon said nothing, seething with fury.

With calm assurance she drove the final nail into the coffin. "Unless, of course, you've squandered too much money away on cards and your family has cut you off. In that case, Godspeed."

She watched his reaction with unfiltered satisfaction. Felicity's information had been a mine of gold, as well as the key to her freedom. When Catherine had learned the staggering amount of debt Simon and John had amassed, and more importantly the names of the powerful men they'd cheated, she knew her days of fearing Simon were over.

Of course, it meant having to reveal herself to him. Years ago when she'd run from him she couldn't ever imagine facing him again. But she was a woman now, with a courage born from love to confront her fears and expel them from her life forever.

"Lastly," she concluded, "you will file no charges of murder against me or anyone else for your brother's death. John was not murdered, Simon. He tripped on his own discarded clothing and dashed his head upon the floor." She shrugged, not about to feign sorrow. "'Tis all that happened."

"It's true." A voice from the doorway filtered into the room. Catherine turned her head and was greeted by the victorious smile of Mrs. Tuckett. She warmed at the sight of her former housekeeper, as if the kindly servant had tucked a blanket around her heart.

Simon's face went purple with rage and he looked

ready to explode like a shot canon. He let out a howl and stormed around the room, sweeping trinkets off the shelves and kicking furniture. He had the crazed look of a rabid animal.

He turned, staring her down, and Catherine's heart jumped into her throat. It took the iron will of a gladiator for her to stand firm, but stand firm she did. She refused to step back or move even an inch as Simon came ever closer.

"You think you can threaten me," he growled. "A murderess whore changing her name and pretending to be someone means nothing. This is my home, *Lucy*, and I do what I want here. Like beating you senseless."

She straightened her spine. "Your violence will not change my mind."

"Perhaps I shall be the judge of that."

She knew he'd expect her to turn chalky white with fear from his threats. Instead, she smiled. "Isn't that just like you to think so? To believe nothing in this world can stop you from doing as you please?"

This time it was Catherine's turn to move forward, and she came close enough to point a finger in Simon's chest. "But you are wrong, Simon, because I am not alone. Two powerful men await me just outside the door, men who could pummel you to jelly in seconds. There are others as well, people who know I am here and who will sound the alarm if I do not return.

"In no time whatsoever, not only will Kingsbridge know of my presence, but all of London. So you see, your threats are merely empty words without meaning. I am the one in charge here, and you will do as I demand or suffer the consequences."

His mouth dropped open as if astounded by what

he heard. Like a deflating balloon, he wilted before her. He turned and walked over to a plush velvet-covered chair, sinking into its depths. He was quiet for a moment and Catherine did not press, giving him time to accept the inevitable. "So if I do not give you what you want..."

"Then I shall ruin you."

He stared straight ahead. Minutes ticked by. "Why?" he asked, his defeated voice little more than a whisper. "Why are you doing this to me?"

At one point in her life, she may have actually felt pity for him. This once vile, domineering man now appeared as a pathetic failure, beaten down by a woman. But he was not to be pitied. Not now, not ever.

"I am doing to you nothing less than what you deserve," she said. "You and your brother lord over women as if they are less than vermin, treating them with wrath and abuse. I tried my best to please your brother and was rewarded only with harsh words and slaps. I asked for nothing except his love, and it was the one thing he never gave me.

"And you, Simon, are exactly like your brother. Mayhap even worse. So you ask why I've done this? You need only look in the mirror for your answer."

His defiance all but gone, Simon merely pressed his lips together and stared.

"You will break off the engagement at once and begin your payments to Felicity. If you do not, I will know, and you shall be reduced to nothing."

The once fearsome man now huddled in his chair. As he closed his eyes, he nodded, agreeing to her request.

She looked away. Her business here was finished.

She would have her freedom. Furthermore, Simon's plan of marrying impressionable young Jane and tormenting her was over. She breathed deeply as she walked outdoors and into the warm, welcoming summer air.

Daylight lingered in the late afternoon. The musical calls of blackbirds and tree sparrows filled the air. A breeze, soft as a lover's caress, drifted over her cheeks. She closed her eyes and inhaled the earthy scents of the English countryside—roses, farmland, towering oak trees—absorbing the familiar smells as if to cleanse herself with them, to wash from her heart the bitter residue of the past.

The soft shuffle of boot heels against the gravel drive drew her attention to where she most wanted to be—in the warm embrace of Miles' arms. Walking toward where he stood beside the carriage, it occurred to Catherine that beginning this new chapter of her life also meant leaving behind a piece of herself, the young girl who'd married and expected love but instead received terror.

That girl no longer existed, replaced by a woman far more worldly, far less trusting. It had taken years of learning to discover the kind of person she wanted to be. She thought the answer was a woman who enjoyed what life had to offer as long as it had not included losing her heart to love. But then...

Miles grasped her outstretched hands and drew her toward him, kissing her with the gentleness of spring rain.

"All is well?" he asked when they finally parted, concern for her etched plainly on his face. "Henry and I watched like hawks through the window. Though it near killed me, we held back as you wanted. But one wrong move and he would have been dead."

She knew the depth of Miles' seriousness by the black look in his eyes. Thankfully, naught had come to pass.

"All is well," she echoed, smiling up at him. "Let's go home."

****

With heartwarming tenderness, Miles guided her backward toward the bed.

He lay her upon it, gently, as if fearful that any undue force would make her shatter like glass. For a moment he simply looked down at her, at her face, in her eyes, his warm, steady breath sweeping across her cheeks. His fingers trailed through her hair and fanned it out upon the pillow. Soft kisses were dotted at her throat before his tongue swept across the tender hollow at her collarbone. She responded at once to his teasing, her nipples stiffening.

"I need to feel you," she murmured, tugging to free his linen shirt from his breeches.

"Not yet." He languidly swiped at her hand as if shooing away a gnat, but Catherine would not be denied.

Slipping her hands in the space between their bodies, her nimble fingers undid the small buttons lining the front of Miles' waistcoat. Once the last one was free she parted the material and pushed it back so she could return her attention to the shirt. She pulled again, this time with more force. In response, Miles placed a hand on either side of her face, tilted it upward, and brought his lips crashing down upon hers.

His kiss was like fire, scorching her everywhere.

He sucked on her top lip, then her bottom. A spear of lust shot through her body. She moaned into his mouth, and he slipped his tongue between her parted lips. Heat like wildfire roared through her veins. She matched the ardor of Miles' kisses with that of her own as her tongue explored the moist heat of his mouth.

When he broke the kiss to focus his attention to her throat, a dam of passion broke free. Low throbs pulsed deep in her core. Her lips parted as she emitted a feral groan.

She arched her back, thrusting her breasts forward, desperate for his caress on her bare skin.

"Now," she demanded, her eyes drifting closed as his palm skimmed over her breast. His low chuckle filtered into the room.

"You're become impatient," he teased.

"Demanding," she corrected, "when there's something I want." She pulled once more at the buttons on his shirt. "And right now, I want you naked."

"You first." A determined glint flashed in his eyes. He sat up and began to remove her clothing.

With practiced fingers he peeled away the layers. She assisted by wriggling on the bed, lifting her hips and back so he could draw the material away until she lay bare before him.

"Your beauty takes my breath away," he murmured as one finger traced a line down the front of her body, from her throat, over her breast, down her stomach. He leisurely drew a circle around her belly button before dipping, just for a moment, over her pelvis to the wet folds of her pussy.

Desire shot through Catherine's body from her nipples to her toes. She sucked in a breath as her thighs parted, craving more of his touch. But he shook his head as he pulled away his finger, tormenting her.

"Nooo," she pouted as her clit throbbed, on fire for him.

"As I recall, you said you wanted me naked." A slow smile slid across his lips as he shrugged off his clothing. He settled himself gently on top of her, his masculine weight pressing her blissfully into the mattress. He kissed her again, at first slowly, tenderly, then with increasing fervor as passion ignited.

There was an urgency in his kiss, Catherine thought, a need that hadn't existed before. She felt it as well. Their lovemaking fulfilled a yearning for her to unite with Miles that went beyond the physical. She wanted to claim ownership, not just of Miles' body but also of his soul. She wanted them to bond with one another—forever.

Miles pulled his mouth away and slid his body down so he could close his lips around her breast, teasing her aching nipple. He sucked hard, and then with his teeth, lightly scraped her nipple before soothing the pleasure-pain with his tongue. She cried out his name as scorching hot lust sizzled through her.

He caressed her entire body while he lavished attention on her breast, his hands gliding over the planes and curves of her hips, her stomach, then delving into the moist flesh between her legs. With deft, practiced movement he sought the place that pleasured her most, teasing and stroking her clit until she writhed beneath him, wantonly arching her hips to increase the pressure of his touch.

Miles plunged one finger then two into the depth of her tight sex, his repeated thrusts mimicking what she'd hoped he'd soon do with his cock. The fleshy part of his hand below his thumb slapped at her clit as he pleasured her.

She moaned, grinding her hips against his hand as her orgasm grew. Release was there, seconds away. Her heartbeat slammed inside her chest. Sweat trickled down her temples as fire roared through her. She squeezed her eyelids shut as she moaned aloud, fingers clutching the bed sheets as she writhed like a courtesan atop the mattress, thrusting hard against Miles' hand. Almost there, almost there...

Release crashed over her, hot, throbbing pulses making her cry aloud. Pinpricks of light exploded beneath her eyelids as the orgasm consumed her, wave after shuddering wave.

Miles held her as she trembled and shook, dotting kisses on her face as she slowly circled down and at last began to still. She opened her eyes, dazzled by the beauty of the man looking down on her.

"Need you now." She lifted her thighs to wrap them around his waist.

He grinned as she slipped one arm around him and pressed a hand against his muscled ass, tilting his hips forward. With her other hand she grabbed hold of his stiff cock, guiding him toward her aching wet pussy.

"Even after all that?"

"*Especially* after all that. You've now whetted my appetite."

His deep chuckle rumbled in the quiet room, mingling with the soft hiss from the candles. But the chuckle transformed into a low groan as she swirled the head of his cock around the wet opening of her sex.

Miles needed no further invitation. He leaned

forward, placing his forearms on either side of her head to support his weight. Then in one swift movement he buried himself in her moist depth, groaning aloud as he withdrew with painstaking leisure before plunging deeply once more.

Catherine twined her arms about his neck to draw their bodies ever closer. But as Miles swept kisses across her cheek, he suddenly stilled, and she knew exactly why. He'd tasted the salt of her tears.

"What troubles you, Catherine?" Concerned tinged his voice. "What is it?"

"'Tis happiness," she replied, hearing her words shake as she whispered them. "These are not tears of sorrow, Miles. They are tears of joy. I..." She took a steadying breath. "I feel as if I am making love for the very first time. I am happy beyond words that I am doing so with you."

"As am I," he said, his voice husky.

She lifted a finger to caress his cheek. "If I could capture a perfect moment and store it in a bottle to savor whenever I wished, this would be that moment."

He began thrusting once more, causing her to sigh deeply with pleasure. "Then let me give you more of those moments," he whispered, "so you never run out of them."

His fingers traveled along her face, dancing upon her lips and cheeks. He leaned down and kissed her deeply, his tongue sliding between her parted lips to explore her mouth. Then he adjusted his pace, plunging his rock hard shaft into her eager pussy with increasing speed, his balls slapping her with every dizzying thrust.

She was rocked with pleasure, his cock stretching and filling her completely. Yet still she wanted more, aching to connect their hearts and souls just like their bodies. She wrapped her arms still tighter around his neck, as if by bringing him closer they would unite as one. He trembled against her and his ragged panting gusted in her ear. She knew he could not deny his release much longer.

The muscles on his sweat-slickened back rippled beneath her palms. She arched her pelvis upward so his thrusts hit her clit exactly right, the rhythmic pounding just what she needed. Her breathing grew quicker and more shallow. Her pulse raced. Miles drove into her three more times, and then her world exploded.

She cried out his name as she shook beneath him, this orgasm even more intense than the one he'd given her only minutes earlier. Miles continued his frenzied pace, his thick shaft pleasuring her until at last she began to calm. Then he thrust twice more, squeezed his eyes shut, and erupted.

When his low groans dissipated at last, he collapsed on top of her. The thumps of his heartbeat vibrated against her chest, and Catherine knew she'd never experienced a more perfect moment, had never felt more alive. The man she loved by her side, his heart beating as one with hers.

When Miles finally rolled off of her, he drew her close by his side, nestling her head in the crook of his arm. With one hand he idly stroked the curve of her hip, back and forth. She shivered beneath his touch, astounded by how easily his soft caress drew out her pleasure, mere minutes after their rapturous union.

After several moments of quiet, Catherine broke the silence. "I am free of Simon," she said, "and other women are safe."

"He agreed not to marry Jane?"

"Nor anyone else."

"And the murder charges against you?"

"He will pursue them no longer."

"You have said goodbye to your past."

"Yes," she agreed. "And I have never been more happy."

He smiled at her, but she was confused as to why it failed to reach his eyes. "Miles?" Her stomach clenched. Something was wrong. "What is it?"

He propped himself on his arm, gazing down at her. "I'm realizing 'tis time," he said softly.

"Time?"

"For you to know my secrets."

She reached her hand up to caress the backs of her fingers against his cheek. "You do not have to tell me."

"I do," he countered. "I need to tell you because I want to cleanse away my demons and set myself free. I want to part ways with the past just as you have done, so I can go on with the future. A future that includes you."

Tears welled in Catherine's eyes and she trembled. What Miles was about to tell her would subject him to reliving an agonizing chapter of his life. When they'd journeyed back from Simon's, she thought perhaps he would share his story. Yet the confrontation with John's brother had emotionally drained her, and Miles had likely sensed the timing wasn't right. She'd needed some distance behind her. Now the moment had arrived.

Miles gathered her close, as if drawing from her the strength to go on. Then he pulled himself away and told her about his past.

"I was married once just as you were," he began. "Although unlike yours, my marriage was good, filled with so much laughter and love. I felt I must be the luckiest man alive."

Catherine could not help the prick of jealousy, like thorns from a rose that stung her even as she admired the happiness Miles once knew.

"Anne and I were married for five years. Our families had known each other for several generations and even when she and I were both children it was assumed Anne and I would one day marry."

"It was arranged, then?"

"Not formally, no. We were both fortunate our parents did not insist on an arranged marriage. It turned out they did not have to for by the time I was one and twenty I knew I was in love with her."

"And she felt the same toward you?"

"She came around eventually." Miles smiled at the memory, but Catherine could see underlying sadness shadowing his eyes and she knew his story would not have a happy ending.

"Once I convinced her to marry me we announced the banns and were wed on a beautiful spring day in May. Shortly more than a year later, we had a child."

Her heart hammered in her chest, afraid to hear the remainder of Miles' story and knowing it was impossible not to. Her breathing reduced to short, shallow breaths as fear began building. Miles had never mentioned a child, and she feared there was a terrible reason why.

"She was a beautiful girl, our Martha," he continued, "always giggling and as full of life as her mother. For the next four years nothing mattered more than my family. Perhaps it was unusual how much I loved those girls, my wife and daughter, but while mates of mine married but kept mistresses on the side, I had no such intention. I had everything I needed right at home. Until the tragedy."

A stray tear slipped down Catherine's face as she began to weep. The grief Miles must have experienced haunted him still; she could see it in his eyes, and now whatever it was, haunted her as well.

"It began with a terrific pain in the back of Anne's head. When I touched her skin it burned, and she raged with fever. The next day it struck Martha. The poor girl cried out from the pain and then became listless as the disease took over. In days they were both covered with pustules."

"The pox," Catherine whispered.

"Yes. In less than a week from whence the disease first began they were gone, passing away within hours of each other." Miles' voice shook, and she was certain it was from the tragic memories assailing him.

"Once they were gone, I wanted to be gone, too. Everything I loved on this Earth had been taken from me. I knew I could not live without them. Driving a stake through my heart would have been less painful than what I endured in the weeks and months following their deaths. I did not leave my home and refused to see anyone. Every person who came to call, whether family or friend, was turned away. I ate nothing. I did not sleep. Grief so consumed me that the only thing I wanted was to be gone from this life. I felt nothing was left."

"Oh, Miles." Catherine sat up in bed and drew her arms around her knees as if to shield herself from the tragedy. Tears streamed down her face as she tried to imagine Miles' catastrophic anguish, so heartbreaking it made him want to end his life.

"Drink was my only friend, because drink was the one thing temporarily blocking the pain. I was deep in my cups for the next six months." He shook his head. "There is irony in that as well, for 'twas likely the only thing that saved me from ending my life was my outrageous drunkenness."

"I don't understand."

He turned to face her, the raw look of tragedy lining his face. "I was far too inebriated to figure out how to do away with myself."

"My God, Miles," Catherine whispered, his anguish striking a chord within her. She knew what it was like to live without hope. "What finally happened? When did you get the strength to live again?"

"From my brother. After six months he'd had enough. One day he came over and told Evans he would not leave without seeing me. My butler agreed but my door was locked and I refused to open it. 'Twas of no concern to Richard for he simply broke it down."

Catherine raised her eyebrows.

"My brother is strong as an ox. You shall see when you meet him."

The promise of that meeting, said so casually, nonetheless filled Catherine with joy. It meant Miles included her in his future.

"Richard saved me that day for he convinced me life was still worth living. He spoke of our family, who had always been close, and he spoke of Anne. She would be devastated to see me how I was, he said, and he was absolutely right. As much as I lost the will to live once she and Martha were gone, I was alive nonetheless and it was time to begin living once more."

"It must have been difficult."

"It was hell," Miles said grimly, "but once I finally reemerged into society, I'd already made a pact with myself concerning any relationships."

"A pact? What was it?"

"I would not love again. Ever."

He made it sound as though it was a pact with the devil. Live, but not love. Exactly the same as what Catherine had done. She realized how tragic the vow sounded once voiced into words.

She, too, had decided never to give love a second chance, thinking her own misery with John was something she could not endure again. She had trusted her heart to someone who had shattered it with humiliation and abuse. Catherine understood something she hadn't before. As long as she upheld her vow never to love, John would continue to defeat her. She had denied herself the one thing she'd always wanted.

Miles turned to Catherine, taking both her hands in his. With heartbreaking tenderness, he leaned forward and kissed her. She felt as if they were sealing a pact of new life with that kiss.

"Everything changed when I met you," Miles continued. "The moment I laid eyes on you, I was lost. Your beauty, your strong will and free spirit, your indifference to being different—you captured me, Catherine. And you saved me."

As she shook her head, he vigorously nodded. "Yes, you did. You saved me. I made that vow to close my heart two years ago. Some months after Richard broke down my door, I started attending social events again, meeting new friends and reacquainting with old ones.

"Eventually, I had physical relations with women but still I did not allow them to touch my emotions. The truth is, none of them had ever come close. The shell around my heart could not be cracked, at least not until you came along and broke it wide open."

Tears flowed down Catherine's cheeks like rain. Her heart swelled, so filled with emotion she thought it would burst. She wrapped her arms around Miles and brought him toward her, basking in his strength and the power of his words as she kissed him.

"You did the same to me," she whispered once they drew apart. "You rescued me from a life filled only with lovers but not with love.

"Once I made the transformation from Lucy Underhill to Catherine Sheffield, I adopted an entirely different lifestyle because I wanted to experience the physical passion between a man and a woman even though I vowed there would never be more than that for me. I do not regret what I've done, for I believe passion should not be forbidden.

"What I did not understand was the love between myself and John—or what I thought was love—in fact was nothing more than a young girl's folly. I never loved John Underhill. I know it now and 'tis thanks to you. You've shown me what love means, Miles. I love you with the very depths of my heart and my soul. I always will."

"My sweet," he murmured, his voice thick with emotion. "'Tis just how I feel. I love you. I love you so much. Every part of you—your heart, your soul, the air you breathe, the life you live. I love all of you.

Forever."

Her heart sang with exuberant joy. Never had she felt this way, as if anything and everything she could ever dream or imagine was possible, all fueled by the strength of Miles' love.

They embraced, sliding down in the bed until they lay flat upon it. Miles propped himself on his arm as he lay beside Catherine so he could lean forward and kiss her lips, and her breasts, and...

"You must marry me," he whispered, capturing her mouth. "I will not stop kissing you until you agree."

"Then I shall not answer." Catherine sighed deeply. "I do not want you to stop kissing me, ever."

The rumble of his laughter vibrated against her chest. Then his voice grew darker and rich with seduction. "But if you agree," he murmured, lowering his head to brush the tip of his tongue across her nipple, "I shall also not stop making love to you. Ever."

He blew air across the tops of her breasts, causing the moisture-laden nipples to stiffen into peaks.

Catherine moaned as desire engulfed her. She opened her eyes to gaze at him. "Do you promise?"

A mischievous grin curved his lips upward and his eyes sparkled. "I promise."

"In that case, I'm yours."

She laughed as Miles drew her body toward him, surrounding her in his embrace and the eternal strength of his love.

About the Author

Elizabeth Shore is a native Wisconsinite and will always consider herself a Cheesehead at heart, but for over fifteen years, New York has been her home.

Elizabeth writes both historical and contemporary erotic romance. She's passionate about Renaissance and Baroque art, classical music, heavy metal, and hockey. She is a devoted animal lover and supporter of animal rights. She's eternally grateful to her husband, Jari, who will always be in her heart.

Visit Elizabeth at
www.LizShore.com

To chat with Elizabeth Shore and other Wild Rose Press authors of erotic romance, join us at
www.groups.yahoo.com/group/thewilderroses.

Also Available

Hot Bayou Nights
by Elizabeth Shore
http://amzn.com/B00J4YVCWI

When corporate consultant Carla Saunders' work takes her from the skyscrapers of Manhattan to a research facility in Louisiana filled with king cobra snakes, she sees her dreams of a job in Paris sinking into the swamp. But unexpected desire burns hotter than a sultry bayou night. The snakes terrify her, but lust for the scorching hot research scientist has her dreaming less about the Champs Élysées and more about being coiled in his arms.

Obsessed with finding a cure for multiple sclerosis, Jackson Rivard's got zero time for relationships. But when a lush, efficient business advisor sweeps into his lab, zero spikes to a hundred before he can shut off the engine. In theory, no-strings-attached sex is scientifically feasible, but having an ex whose fangs make a cobra's seem modest brings new meaning to the phrase "once bitten, twice shy." How can he protect his heart when Carla's charming it out of hiding?

Also Read

Time for a Highlander
Real Men Wear Kilts
by Maxine Mansfield
http://amzn.com/B01BHG8318

Forty-five-year-old history teacher Bethany Anne Anderson wasn't supposed to die on her dream vacation to Scotland. Someone else was supposed to rescue the child from the falling druid stone. But she's perfectly fine with moving on to the hereafter. She has loved ones waiting for her. Then Tobias Morie, better known as Fate, steps in. Her intervention has changed the future. Before she can move on, she must first help him correct one of his own mistakes. That's fine until she wakes up in 1643 in the body of twenty-year-old Lady Elspeth Frasier. Worse, she's engaged to the very handsome, very young, very virile Quinton MacLeod. But that's not all Fate demands. She must give the Highland laird the heir he'd originally been denied.

Quinton MacLeod loved once. He won't do it again, even if he had time for such nonsense. With the Highland lairds divided between loyalty to their beloved country and the English king, he seeks only peace—in his keep and in his heart. But raised in England and a ward of the enemy, his beautiful new wife has strange notions of education and cleanliness that cause chaos within both. There's also the matter of her very unlady-like views on the marriage bed, which, come to think of it, he's more than happy to overlook. If only he could trust her.